The Covert Peace

By: Darnell Denzel Williams

with Tara N. Woolfolk, Ph.D.

authorHOUSE®

AuthorHouse™
1663 Liberty Drive
Bloomington, IN 47403
www.authorhouse.com
Phone: 1-800-839-8640

First published by AuthorHouse   06/02/2011

ISBN: 978-1-4567-4679-7 (sc)
ISBN: 978-1-4567-4683-4 (dj)
·ISBN: 978-1-4567-4680-3 (ebk)

Library of Congress Control Number: 2011904142

Printed in the United States of America

This book is dedicated to all the wonderful people who helped inspire me to chase my dreams and while this list will never fully cover all the people. I am forever humbled for every ounce of support.

Special Thanks

Tonya & Calvin (My Parents)
You have raised me from a wide eyed cry baby, to a think I know it all teen and now to a young adult filled with gratitude and undying appreciation. I am blessed to have wonderful parents like you and without the love you have provided me I would have never accomplished this task, so I say thank you.

Dr. Tara Woolfolk
I came to Rutgers with a broken backpack, an unreadable schedule, and more debt to my name than I could ever imagine. Despite my confusion I had one thing and that is hope. You believed in me, and I cannot fathom the completion of this book without your profound insight and for that I am forever indebted to you.

Mama Dukes (Hourigan/Hampton Family) & Kelly Briggs/Family
You all took in a broke college kid with nothing but hopes and dreams. I set out on my own adventure to find my place in this world, and you all provided me with a roof over my head. It was difficult making a transition from moving out of my parent's house, but with open arms and love you made sure I had a place to rest my head. I love you all and thank you for watching over me.

Castillo/Lugo/Vicente Family

Since day one when I announced I wrote a book you guys were instrumental in the development. You all seemed to be more determined to get this thing published than I was. I would have never known the next step without you guys. I love you all. Here is too many more to come.

Alyssa, Lindsey, Melissa, Teresa

A simple hello can shape destinies. When we are uncertain as to why things happen the way they do that is fate working. I have gained a small sense of what struggles lie behind inner beauty, love and self acceptance. But ultimately I have discovered the power of altruism and how it may lead to everlasting peace. Because of you I am able to share these lessons and as the old adage goes *for every life touched that life touches another.* My deepest love to all of you, and here is to you.

Ms. Evbuoma, Ms. Renda, Mrs. Robertazzi, Ms. Merolla, Ms. Lopez Mr. LaVeglio, Mr. Johnson, Mr. Newell & Mr. Wilson

Thank you all for being mentors to me as I work to become a teacher. Each of you has instilled in me a passion and a drive into becoming an effective teacher. Teaching is a performance and you're on a stage. You are the writer/performer. The administrators are your editors. The students are your audience, and the critics are the communities hoping for the best show they could have ever dreamed. No pressures. No worries. And Mr. Wilson points at me and asks, "Darnell do you believe in yourself," I reply, "Yes, I believe in me." Thank you all.

My Students

You all did nothing more than believe in me. It kept me motivated. Never forget to work hard and fight for what you believe in. You are dynamite. You are out of sight.

"May we all reach peace in our lives and be able to find, keep and cherish the things that give us our serenity."

CONTENTS

Prologue

The Envelopes

"So do you think people can change?" He asked, trying to keep pace with how fast Covey was walking.

"Well, with the right encouragement and understanding I would like to believe that people can change." Covey reached into his pocket and pulled out two thick envelopes.

"What's in there?"

Covey answered with one word, "Hope."

"Well can I see it?" Covey handed him the envelopes. He went to open it, but Covey put his hands over it and shook his head.

"You will know when you can open it."

"Okay . . . well can you at least tell me where we are going?"

"We're not going anywhere she will come to us."

He was about to ask another question, but Covey raised his hand in the air. He tapped him on the shoulder and pointed him to look up ahead. The younger boy looked up to see where Covey was pointing. Up ahead all he could see was a group of girls wearing red graduation gowns. The one in the middle was exchanging laughs with the other two who seemed to giggle louder with each passing step. The girl in the middle had layered blond hair and a beautiful appearance. As the girls came closer to passing the boys, the girl in the middle suddenly stopped her laughing when she saw Covey. They made direct eye contact and time seemed to freeze. The girls passed Covey and the younger boy. They never spoke a word to each other. They never bumped shoulders. They appeared to glide right past each other without missing a beat. The girl and Covey looked back at the same time after a few short steps separated them. Covey gave a meaningful smile and a wink of the eye. Her dark eyes lit up and she smiled as she turned the corner and continued her journey.

"What was that about?" The boy asked curiously.

"That was her moment of serenity." Covey turned back to the boy and smiled. He stopped in his tracks. He looked at the younger boy and asked, "Have you ever made a wish?"

The question was followed by an awkward silence. The boy stared at him perplexed. "Yeah, a few years ago I made a wish." He fixed his lips to say something else, but Covey stopped him.

"You're not supposed to tell someone what you wish for otherwise it won't come true. Come on now after all these years I would think you would have learned that by now. Nevertheless here is our stop. I have to go now." Before Covey turned around and started to walk away, he paused. The boy held the envelope firm in his hands staring down at the ground. A breeze swept a full-green leaf across the boy's feet and onto the headstone from which Covey read aloud, "Our moment of life does not begin when we spread our wings, but rather when we see the beauty of soaring over the horizon." He turned and walked away.

"Hey Covey," he screamed out breaking the whispers of the wind. He stopped, but he never turned around. The younger boy continued, clutching the envelopes in his hands. "Thank you for everything."

"You're welcome Little Bear."

*   *   *

Little Bear sat down on the first empty park bench he could find. He turned the envelopes over in his hands for a tenth time before he dared to open it. His conversation with Covey was fresh in his mind, yet at the same time he almost wondered if he imagined it. He thought about the last thing he had heard at the graveyard from Covey. "Our moment of life does not begin when we spread our wings, but rather when we see the beauty of soaring over the horizon." He thought, who said that? It seemed so impossible somehow. But he knew the words Covey spoke were real and could not forget them. Taking one last deep breath, he began to open the first envelope, and wondered aloud. "Why me? I'm just another 16-year old boy. Wasn't there someone else who should be doing something that seemed so important? But all he knew was, he made Covey a promise to share these envelopes with the world, and he was going to keep it. He pulled out the neat pile of papers from the first envelope and began to read them . . . .

*   *   *

CHAPTER 1—The Empty Bus Seat

(Harvey, IL)

November 3, 2008

(Girl 1)

Dear Journal,

I don't know what just happened. It was surreal. When he spoke I blacked out, but I heard everything he was saying. It was like I had left my body and was floating near the ceiling—like I was watching my own life play out like a movie. When he touched my head I broke down and started to visualize all the horrible things that have happened to me in my life. I saw people teasing me throughout my whole life in school, and saw me cry myself to sleep every single night begging for God to just kill me. I saw my parent's divorce, and how my best and only friend left me when I needed him the most. I didn't know then that he wasn't what he seemed to be. That "friend" was nothing but a druggie, a drunk and a liar; he was nothing but a horrible person. But right then, he was my BEST friend, and I needed him. I saw how much of a scumbag my mom's boyfriend was to her, and how he tried to touch me when I was only twelve. I even saw all the times in my life that I was told I wouldn't amount to anything and that I should just go and commit suicide, which I have thought about for as long as I can remember, but only attempted once. My mind went back to all the teachers that said I would never amount to anything, and made me feel I wasn't good enough.

Then all my thoughts came back to the present as he continued, "You have been touched by an angel." And I believe I was. At that moment I snapped out of my trance like state; I saw him walk away into the darkness. He left me with a job to do, and I attempted it. This led me to writing this entry. I wish he were standing in front of me, so I can just hug him and say thank you.

Indeed, he has shown me something no one else ever has before this. He has shown me that I am not what those people have said to me, or the things they did. He showed me they were all just mere instances in my life, and that in a way, they even helped me. They molded me into the beautiful person I am. He helped me see that I am worth something. He impacted me in an entirely different way than anyone else has; a directly positive one. He told me I was worth something, no matter what anybody else said and that he was proud of me. This is something I have heard before, but it was in exchange for things like getting good grades or taking out the trash on time. This time was different. He had no reason to say that to me. I hadn't done anything for him. All I did was sit there and listen to him. He agreed to come out here to talk to me today and it's something I will never forget.

I know that one conversation will not change my entire life overnight. But I have hope now. And even though I'm not sure how long it will be before he steps out of my life, this will never truly leave me. It will always be a part of me, because it showed me a light that has never shined on me. I hope my light stays.

She let her mind wander back to August, that same year . . . .

*   *   *

Little Bear paused for a moment, and thought about what he had just read. He didn't know this girl, but he hoped her light would stay too. Wondering why she was thinking of August at a time like this, he pondered what life must have been like before she wrote this entry. So far, he was fascinated, if a little confused.

*   *   *

August 13, 2008

(About four months earlier)

Once again bus 177 was running behind the normal "three o'clock on the dot" schedule. As the kids from the forgotten about projects of Harvey dreaded the summer's heat many of them began to fuss. Their frustration seemed echoed by their collective rough appearance. The I.D.'s that were worn around their necks were said to be "safety measures," but the five digit numbers etched under their names did not seem to separate them from the markings on the clothing of criminals. The security guards stationed near the exit doors had their holsters lined with flashlights, a nifty pad that came clipped with a pen, and walkie-talkies that only picked up only one channel. Their only real purpose was to keep the gangs separated from each other. Every student seemed to have their own place of belonging. With a quick glance one could see who belonged to what gang family, who was part of the band, or even who stood alone.

The person who stuck out most from the crowd was the young lady with so many books; some had to be held in her arms tucked snug between her crossed arms and chest. The others were in her fully stuffed backpack. She seemed awkward, uncomfortable with her nearly six feet of height. She seemed to curl up a bit so that she might blend in with the shorter girls. Her body was full figured from waist side to back side. The hoodie she wore, and others whispered that she was crazy for wearing one in the heat, was faded black and its hood strings were annoyingly uneven, squashed between chest and the calculus textbook she held tiresomely. Her legs were free to breathe as the extra baggy jeans stretched all the way to her toes housing them ever so freely. The irritated face was justified by the perspiration that formed on her forehead. Her dark glasses covered her eyes, but the biting of her bottom lip and creased eyebrows made them pierce fiercely through the lenses. Red cheeks and a flared nose added to the awkwardness and intimidation to even approach her. Her long dark brown hair was tucked behind her ears and extended down her back a few inches or so past her shoulders. No one stood near, as if someone had drawn a five feet boundary around her. Her intense breathing was due to her sinuses, so a steady hum was generated from her mouth and out through her chapped lips.

Finally, the bus rolled in loudly and pulled in front of the sixty kids angrily waiting to go home. That young lady made sure she was the first to grab her seat. She sat five seats on the left side always behind the bus driver. She scooted as close as her body would allow her to the window, and glazed aimlessly while waiting for the rest of the people to board. She began to think about papers she had to write, the calculus that needed to be completed and tried to figure out what she would be having for dinner, because like always, mom would be working until late. Her thoughts of self-pity were interrupted when she glanced to her right and noticed her empty seat had been occupied. This face was unfamiliar, and never had anyone sat next to her before. Her glance became an awkward stare.

His handsome smile was not weakened by the strength of her glare. His appearance was striking, but not as much as the aura that seemed to fill the atmosphere in his presence. The awkward gaze ended abruptly when eye contact was made between the two. To her surprise the stare was met with an inviting smile. As she fought not to startle at his continuing stare she could not help peering into his unwavering eyes. She shifted her head back to the left where she resumed looking out the window.

As the bus made each routine stop through the rinky-dink town she frantically peeked to her right to see which stop was his. With a few blocks to go before her stop on 150th street the bus came to a stop at the corner of 147th and he swiftly got off and walked into the distance. The bus pulled up at a stop sign, tagged "FREE ME" on 150th street, and as she prepared to get up she realized she had been holding her breath the entire time since he had gotten off. She exhaled in frustration, gathered her calculus book and backpack and headed down the bus aisle.

While walking through the trailer park on this day she didn't even notice the boarded up trailers, the cracks that lined the uneven sidewalks, or even the stench that filled the air. All of her focus was locked in on her bus seat five rows back on the left hand side as she began to hope the unfamiliar face she had instantly grown intrigued by would occupy the empty bus seat.

*   *   *

A passing breeze caught Little Bear's attention momentarily. Off in the distance Little Bear could see that the sun was rising higher in the sky. The sun seemed almost unbelievably perfect that day. He half smiled thinking of the girl on the bus' light and he wondered what was to come, seeing that the next part of the packet contained another address and entirely different date . . . .

*   *   *

Chapter 2—Mirror Image

(New York)

December 14, 2008

(Girl 2)

Hey Covey,

Wow! I am so sorry it has taken this long. Things can get pretty crazy, huh? Well, as you have probably guessed I have rewritten this letter about 10 times. I want it to be perfect. Alright, I am going to explain how much of an impact you have had on me. We only chilled for like, three days at most, and with our conversations you would have never known it. You'd think we've known each other forever. Right from the start you have been there for me 100%—scratch that, 110%. I always know when I am feeling at my low I can turn to you. I have poured so much into your hands, and you have poured it all right back into mine with so much more light and positive attitude; enough positive attitude to put an even bigger smile on my face. You have helped me realize what being a strong person is really about. You've helped me realize that being strong isn't being able to put on a show for everyone. It's about being able to show the emotions you are feeling right at that moment. It's about taking everything from the past, good and bad, and being able to hold them by your side and not so much be ashamed, but somewhat proud of whom you are. It is about being able to move on with your life and not let your past tear you down, but to look at the positive in the obstacles that you have overcome, the ones you are over coming and the ones you are bound to surmount.

Now, my past isn't as bad as some people's, but I've been through my dad leaving us for the woman across the street when I was four. I went from daddy's little girl to therapy within such little time. My family was in a rut for three years; my brother and I pretty much had to take care of ourselves. I was anorexic and cutting myself by the 6th grade. I was cutting up until about the 10th grade, and it is something I have not been able to let go of, and to this day I still get urges. By the time I was in the 9th grade I became bulimic, and once again it is something I cannot let go of. I overdosed on 26 Advil pills going into the summer of my 10th grade year. All because my grandmother was someone I had always cherished and it was unbearable watching her suffer for so long at such a young age. I guess God had seen enough and took her out of this world in February. I think losing her and our house in a recent flood was part of the reason the family did become closer. The taking four years of my ex-boyfriend's mental and physical abuse didn't work well for me either. He has beat the hell out of me, but even through all the pain am I a fool to love him and believe that things will get better?

Despite all that has happened to me in the last four years I have gotten better. That night when you made me look into the mirror is the moment when everything changed. That night really helped me find myself and become more secure. I have always prayed for God to help me when I was stuck. I think he has finally given me that help, and that was **YOU**! I can honestly say to you that you are a best friend. I mean it with all I have that when I hear your voice, whether in a time of need or not, I have a secure feeling; just because I know you care. You are my hero. You make it a part of your duty to help anyone who needs it. You are the nicest person I have ever met, not to mention the most caring. You have the biggest heart out of **<u>EVERYONE</u>** I know. Well, I just thought I would let you know all of that. I love you lots and lots it is profound and only we will ever be able to understand!

Love Me Forever!

*   *   *

That last letter sounded all too familiar. Little Bear stopped and looked away from the packet for a good long minute. It was almost like he was reading about part of his own life. Was it a mere coincidence that some of the struggles that the girl mentioned matched parts from when he was ten? He shook it off and continued to read, compelled to find out what would happen next . . . .

*   *   *

August 8, 2008

(About 5 months earlier)

She tied her long black hair and dabbed the silent tears that rolled down her cherubic cheeks. The dark rings around her eyes still existed, but the make-up made her seem as if she were only tired. Her stare became a hopeless glaze as the image that reflected a fake and forced smile began to fade. Her beautiful fair skin now resembled a purple and green shade. Her eyes never shined anymore, and her eyelids hung low and dreary. Her eyelashes were long and elegant, but only served as a distraction from her own vision. The lines across her wrist were perfect red parallel lines. After a long stare in the mirror she untied her hair and let it flow loosely around the bruises on her neck. She took the hair tie and rolled it onto her wrist. *Much better*, she thought to herself.

As she made her way down the stairs she counted her steps. The ten steps that led directly into the living room were steep, so she cautiously held on to the railing. She wasn't used to such steep steps. She wasn't used to a living room that was filled with what seemed to be happy family portraits. She tried not to be jealous as she looked at the picture of the big happy family who smiled so freely. She was only going to be there for a few short weeks. The flood had ruined their basement at home and they were not allowed back in, so her mom sent her to stay with the Leyo's.

She plopped down on the loveseat and waited for Niya. She and Niya grew up together in New York, but once Mr. Leyo got a promotion the family moved to New Jersey. Niya was always overly nice. She seemed to be oblivious to the things that were happening all around her. She loved Niya's outlook on life, but wished her friend could just listen to her problems rather than always think that things would just magically get better. Niya came prancing in the room with a cheerful good morning. Niya's life seemed to be a musical playing in her head. Niya lifted her from the loveseat and she followed her out of the door.

The girls walked to McDonald's, which to her seemed a million miles away because the rain was coming down in buckets. Of course Niya danced and twirled on the sidewalks the entire way. As she watched Niya and tried to lighten up a car drove by near the curb splashing water all over her. The second the girls walked in she ran into the bathroom. Her makeup was now almost melting all over her face. She opened her purse and pulled out her makeup kit. As she applied her makeup she took a good look at herself. She was disgusted at her droopy eyes and the light bruises that stained her face. She used her fingers as a final touch to smooth the rest of the cover up and slowly walked out of the bathroom.

She was surprised as she returned to her seat that someone was seated next to her friend. Niya waved her arms frantically, telling her to hurry up to the seat. She sat down across from the stranger and he gave her a calm smile.

"This is Covey," Niya said excitedly, "and he has been helping me out with all my silly problems.

He then turned to her friend, "I know I do not really know the first thing about you, but any friend of hers is a friend of mine. Anything you need you just let me know. I am here for you as well. Never be afraid to call on me."

She half smiled at what somehow seemed to be a serious offer. The guy almost seemed like he had a light shining just on him, even on such a dark and dank day. She pondered if he could see right through her dark eyes. She used her hands to comb her hair over and slowly slid them under the table. Her sense of security was regained.

He scooted out of the chair without making a sound. He smiled one last time before he walked out of the door. With a graceful wave of his hand he vanished into the rainy scenery. In three days he would be moving on.

August 15, 2008

She had the phone in her hand. She had attempted the call five times now. The seven digits were already embedded in her memory. The first ring happened so fast she quickly hung up. She couldn't help but wonder what would he say; let alone what would he think? What was she to say? She practiced the phone call over and over again. "Um, hey it's me," she started to speak out loud, but that would sound foolish. The frustration swelled deep in her brain. Just then her fingers pressed redial. With each beep of the number her stomach dropped further and she collapsed on her bed. The phone cord had become wrapped around her ankles from her constant pacing and she did not even realize her footprints were now traced in her cream carpet. Just when she was going to press the end button to unravel herself she heard the light breathing on the other end. Before she could force herself to end the call she found to her surprise that she would be the first to speak.

"You told me I could call on you," her voice cracked in a low whisper.

"Yes, I did say that."

"So, now what am I supposed to do?"

"At this point you don't have to say anything else. I just want you to listen to my voice and what I have to say. Tonight I have a challenge for you. I took the same challenge and it helped me out. I want you to look into the mirror for an entire minute. It sounds like a short time, but it feels like forever. Here is the catch though; you are looking past your physical features and into your own eyes. I want you to look deep into your soul. Think about every moment that has had a drastic impact on your life. Recall all the hidden pain, all the built up hatred, all those who doubted you, and every night you wanted nothing more than to give up, but didn't. It is okay if the tears come out. Tonight you will start to find yourself. After you complete this challenge then give me a call, and together we will start to help you grow and love, again. I am going to hang up now. Good night."

The phone fell out of her hands onto the floor. Her mind began to race frantically. What could he possibly be talking about? How could someone look past their physical features if they were the main thing reflected? She stood in front of the mirror with her eyes closed. There was much shame and guilt that filled her heart. When she finally gained enough strength to open her eyes she was startled by her own reflection. Her face resembled a NASCAR racetrack as all of her mascara had smeared across her face leaving trails of black streaks. The bruises on her face no longer blended magically with the foundation and cover up. She could not avoid staring helplessly at her own pathetic image—it was as if she couldn't even find her eyes to look into. His voice began to echo in her head again, so she slowly forced herself to look into her big black eyes. From that point on there was no turning back. The mirror started to reflect her life's journey in her eyes, and she reminisced in her own thoughts of confusion. A new journey was about to begin for her, and it filled her with hope.

*   *   *

Little Bear couldn't believe it. He held the papers in his hands and tried his best to make sense of all of this. But there was no doubt that this girl was indeed his sister. Flustered by all this he moved on to the next part of the envelope . . .

*   *   *

CHAPTER 3—Her Little Secret

(Midlothian, IL)

January 13, 2009 8:03 a.m

(Girl 3)

I was raped as a child by someone in my family. I went to counseling, but I almost feel like it couldn't have happened to <u>me</u>. Then later, I dated a boy from Indiana when I was thirteen. He abused me and raped me when I tried to break up with him. We broke up, so I got away. But I still got pregnant and I have kept it a secret from my family the whole time. Now I have a child that is going to turn three. Her name is Lillian Love and my parents don't even know about her. Now you know my story.

*   *   *

The last letter gave Little Bear a chill. He couldn't even fathom a young girl having a baby and keeping it a secret for such a long time. He thought how could something like this even happen? Besides all that, why was he chosen to read these stories? Little Bear knew there had to be more to this story. The letter was so short compared to the others. He hoped there was another letter that followed so he could understand more . . . .

When Little Bear glanced at the next sheet to see if it was written by the same girl, he found that it was typed. This seemed odd, among all the hand written pages. And there was no name on it like the others. Who could have written this? He hoped as he read more, it would make more sense to him.

*   *   *

(no date)

When I finished the letter, I looked up and she had already faded away into the crowd. I folded the note up and put it in my pocket. Somehow I managed to rearrange my shock and put a smile on. She had reached out to me for help and I was going to be there for her. I could not help but wonder how she had come so far with such a secret. I would forever call her My Wonder.

*   *   *

Hmm, thought Little Bear, aloud. Who the heck wrote that? And WHEN did he write it? Could someone else have been able to read this stack of papers before him? He was almost ready to stop reading until he solved this mystery. But as a light breeze blew by, it lifted the top sheet enough for him to recognize the handwriting of the girl whose letter had just left him with 101questions. For now he pushed the rest out of his mind, and read on.

∗   ∗   ∗

January 13, 2009

She had observed him for months now. His presence was like no other. He had sat next to her in psychology class. He was sociable and could draw a crowd from just his voice alone. She had decided this would be the day she would reach out to him.

When she walked in he was already prompt and in his seat. He was shining and his smile was glistening as he spoke to other peers. She flashed a smile to him and mouthed the words good morning.

On this day she was covered from head to toe. Her zebra designed scarf was wrapped around her neck and hung low to the ground. Her hair was tightly tied back and two pencils kept her bun in place. Her black socks were worn on the outside of her jeans extended all the way up to her knees. Her white shirt was a perfect fit and her shoes were laced tightly.

She took her seat next to him. Class proceeded and just before 8:00 a.m she handed him the very note that would change her life. She slipped it on his desk when he scurried off to hand in the class work before the bell rang. He returned and opened the note. The red ink was fresh across the paper, and it looked as if it had been written in the dark.

∗   ∗   ∗

Well, he wasn't sure how much more he had learned, but at least now he knew who that short letter came from. Sure enough, the next page was graced with a different person's handwriting. He shook his head, feeling tired, but yet too intrigued to stop reading on . . . .

*　　*　　*

CHAPTER 4—The Runaway

(Portland, Oregon)

March 31, 2009

(Girl 4)

Dear Covey,

The other night you told me to ask myself "why me," and I didn't know how to answer it. To be honest, I still don't really know. I know how to write my feelings on paper rather than saying them out loud, and I guess that's why I am writing this. I guess in order to really understand why I feel like I can tell you all this, I must fill you in on what I have been through and what I'm going through. The things that have happened to me are, like, straight out of a movie . . . well, some are amazing, and some are the worst things you could fathom. I am not sure where to start, but I guess the beginning is the best place to start things off.

Well, I was born on December 1, 1992. My mother gave me the name Serenity. I was born with blond hair, black eyes, and fair skin. They say my daddy knew when he first held me that I would be a dancer and a leader.

As I got older, pretty, taller and more independent, feelings between my mom and dad got intense. When I was five years old my parents got divorced, and from my childhood that is what I remember most.

I was sicker than I could ever recall being in my young life. I was watching television and listening to my mom sing in cook in the kitchen. My daddy swung the door open and started yelling words I didn't understand at the time. My daddy was never the type to hit a woman, but I heard a slam against the wall, and a pot of boiling water fall hit the floor. I knew something wasn't right when I walked in and saw my mother's feet against the wall and hovering above the ground. Her face was pale and drained of color. Her eyes were burning red and her lips dripped fresh blood that flowed down her chain and neck. I screamed and asked my daddy what he was doing? He said nothing. He put her down, gave her a kiss on the cheek, and as she laid on the floor in her own misery he packed his suitcase and walked out of the door.

I ran out the door to see where he was going, but he was already half way out of the driveway. I ran after him as fast as I could go begging and screaming, please don't leave. I know for a fact that he saw me as his eyes caught mine through the rearview mirror. But he never stopped. At the end of my block you could turn left out of town or turn right towards the school and houses. That day my daddy turned left and I went right. I sprinted to my school and slept in the tunnel slide that night. When I finally returned home my mother was still in the fetal position only this time her eyes were dried and the blood stains etched the floor like dried up red wine. It was at that time I felt I had to take care of my own mother. I couldn't even look at myself in the mirror because all I saw in my face was him. Three years later he returned. I recognized him from what only seemed to be a nightmare, but I forgave him and now we have become closer than ever.

In 1999, for my own good, my mom sent me to move in with my auntie in Portland, Oregon. Of course the Blazers are now my all-time favorite team. I lived right next to the Rose Garden and October 16, 1999 will always be the best day in my life. My cousin Aiden and I had got in trouble with my uncle. He was furious because we had got caught stealing from a store. We were really hungry, so we went to Seven-Eleven and stole a bag of chips. I didn't think it was that big of deal, but my uncle did. He didn't like me hanging around Aiden because he was so much older than I was. Aiden was 17, had dropped out of school and spent most of his days fighting with my uncle. I know it sounds bad, but Aiden was still cool with me. He had this way with people. He introduced me to all his older friends and he promised that he would always take care of me. After we got caught stealing, my auntie made us stay in the room until my uncle got home. Not even five minutes after she left Aiden opened the window and told me to follow him.

We ended up at the Rose Garden. We snuck in through the back entrance. It was amazing. The gym was huge. I ran to the center of the court looking in awe. Aiden was smiling and said, "pretty cool, huh?" It was like being on a grand stage, and the floors were so squeaky clean you could see part of your reflection. Aiden came over as I was admiring my surroundings and told me that he came here every so often to escape from the world. He took off a small silver ring he had being wearing. He told me it was his good luck charm and he would only wear it when he felt he needed it the most. He told me to keep it because he knew I needed it more.

That changed my whole perspective on things in this world. He knew I had been through a lot. He knew I needed something to keep me going; a little something personal to keep forever. I still have that ring, but I only wear it when I am afraid or just want to escape from this world. It shines with beauty right now. I never saw Aiden again after that day. He ran away from home.

I have lost the one person in the world who means the world to me. Aiden was my cousin and my best friend. He shot himself August 8, 2008. I lost the last person who had ever stuck by my side. He gave me everything I ever wanted; he was my best friend, my cousin, and my mentor. Everything I do is for him; every serve in volleyball, every pitch in softball, and every dance step. All I want is my cousin back. I never even got a chance to say good bye. He taught me how to always set my goals high, and you have reinforced it!

Someday . . .
I will grow up
Someday . . .
I will graduate from college
Someday . . .
I will own my own beauty shop
Someday . . .
I will meet Barack Obama
Someday . . .
I will have my own beautiful family
Today . . .
I will change the world.
Covey, I have no idea why things work the way they do, but I LOVE YOU!
FOREVER AND ALWAYS!

*   *   *

Little Bear thought to himself, "That poor girl." He recalled what it felt like to lose someone in his family. These four girls all seemed hurt and lost, but yet Little Bear knew that there had to be much more to these stories. He shifted in his seat and took a glance at his watch. It was just before 4 in the afternoon and now the rays from the sun were shining brightly upon him. He flipped over to the next page, but not without first thinking what these girls shared in common and what became of the first girl he read about. He could see his curiosity was about to be satisfied when he saw that the next page was typewritten.

*   *   *

Chapter 5—Occupied Seat

(Harvey, IL)

August 15, 2008

(Girl 1)

    She counted each seat slowly in her head. She reached her seat. It was untouched as always. She slid in and sat all the way towards the window. It had been another long day, and she was happy that it had finally come to an end. Her thoughts began to sweep over her again. Just then she felt something overcome her entire body. It was that new presence she had felt briefly before. She had been facing the window, and knew when she turned to her right he would be sitting there. She turned her head slowly. There he was.

    His amazing smile gleamed with beauty. He flashed off his impressive teeth and nodded his head. He looked down at his papers and began to shuffle them back together. It came to a surprise to both of them when she spoke.

    "Why are you sitting here?" Her words were stinging, but unintentionally so. She had no idea whether to be sorry for her words, bitter at his response, or just start over with no spoken words at all. There were no take backs.

"Hello, I am sorry. Were you saving this seat for someone else? My name is Covey, and I am new to town, I . . ."

"I didn't ask for your name or who you are," she abruptly interrupted. "You are in my seat."

"Well, would you like me to move?" His patience was fading, but yet his smile remained.

In her mind she thought of how sweet his voice truly was. How she didn't want him to leave. How she couldn't believe this incredible feeling he was giving her. She wondered where he had been. The roads he had traveled. She pictured spending time with him. No worries. No problems. All the neglect, all the long nights and all the hell seemed to fade in her thoughts just from his mere presence. She could not help but wonder just one more thing. Perhaps it was her defense mechanism or maybe just a legit thought, but even with all of the good feelings, still the question remained in her mind. Why was he being so nice to her?

She quickly glanced at his face. Before she could answer his question he interrupted her thoughts, feelings, and what seemed to be her last hope.

"Well, this is my stop. I am sorry. I will not sit in your seat anymore."

By the time she had snapped out of her trance he was gone, again. She had to be sure the next time she saw him she would not ruin it.

The bus pulled up to 150th street and she gathered her books and headed off. She missed him already. His name was Covey. What an unusual name, she thought. She walked into her home and went straight to her room. She locked the door behind her. His name continued to ring hopefully in her head.

August 18, 2008

Finally, the three o'clock bus had come. It arrived late as usual, but she still was the first one on. She counted each seat until she reached five. She scooted all the way in towards the window and waited.

Covey walked on the bus ten minutes after she did. She fought back her small urge to smile and waited for him to walk towards her. He never did. He sat directly behind the bus driver. No one sat next to her. Her seat had once again become empty. As her smile faded away her eyes began to well up with tears. The bus continued through the run-down towns. When the bus reached his stop she peered up through her dark lenses, and watched him fade away into the distance. She was lonely.

August 29, 2008

Her seat had remained empty for days now. Every day she watched him repeat his same old ways. He never looked back. She had not seen his smile or even felt his presence. Her hope was slowly dwindling away.

When the bus reached her stop she got off slowly and dreaded each step towards her house. Today her power was out. Mom didn't have enough money to keep up with the bills. She hoped the water would be hot again by the time the warm days began to turn cool into the fall season.

Her father came to visit on this day. The moment he walked in the door she went into her room and locked the door and waited until he was gone, like she always did. Once again he was drunk and his reckless talking reverberated off the walls. His size was daunting. The tattoo that etched his skin was that of a woman who seemed to be frightened severely. His balding gave him an even angrier look as they were accompanied by his tired eyes. He approached his daughter's door. He banged on her door with small, strange laughter in his voice.

"Open this damn door and come out and give your daddy a kiss!"

"No, why don't you just leave me alone. I don't wanna see you!"

"You are worthless just like your mother. You're weak and you'll never survive. I am leaving!"

The tears were uncontrollable at this time and her voice cracked as she screamed back, "I don't care!"

His footsteps echoed down the small hall. The front door slammed so loud it shook the entire trailer. She cried out to God begging Him to just take her life, now. She flopped down on her bed that was made up of one mattress and two sheets. The only thing that gave her single bed a little style was her stuffed animals, some petite and some larger. She reached for her favorite one, Winnie the Pooh. He filled one of her arms. Taped on his red shirt was a picture of her and her father, from when she was five years old. She was sitting on his lap and he had his arms wrapped around her tightly while kissing her on the forehead. It was one of the happiest times in her life. In fact it was the last time she remembered her smile being real. She flipped Winnie over and lifted up his red shirt. Stuffed within her bear was her diary. She pulled out her diary and began to write. She wrote one thing in it. In big letters spread across the page she wrote WHY.

September 29, 2008

Three o'clock came and when the bus finally arrived she bum rushed everyone out of the way. One, two, three, four, and five she counted in her head and she took her seat. At this point in time she cared for no one. It was only fair because no one cared for her. Today she was going to end all of her pain. No more worries after today. She repeated it over and over in her head.

She glared out the window. The leaves on the trees had faded to burnt brown and orange colors. The cool breeze gently pulled the leaves off the trees and the seemed to bounce them in the air and sway them quietly towards the ground. Once a leaf hits the ground it becomes a burden, she thought. It's to be raked up, bagged up, and tossed away. The leaf becomes useless. The tree would be naked and free with no worries because new leaves would come. Every leaf would be picked up by the wind only to be let down. New leaves will grow and replace those old leaves thrown to the ground. The tree would be beautiful again, but no one will ever worry about the leaves that used to be.

As she watched the leaves float down to their ends she felt something sweep over her body. Her cheeks immediately flushed red. She couldn't help but look to her right. There he was. Covey stood in front of her with his smile and a glisten in his eyes.

"Hello, I know you do not want me to sit in your seat, but it appears someone beat me to the seat in which I normally sit. Do you mind if I sit here for today?"

Her mood shifted dramatically. She wanted to jump up for joy. She wanted nothing more than for him to sit. To listen to his soothing voice for hours. She did not want to ruin this opportunity this time.

"Well, Covey is it? I never told you that you had to move the first time," her words were spoken sarcastically. "You never let me answer your question from before, but since I am in a good mood you may sit."

Covey sunk into the seat. He shuffled through some papers in his hand and then gently placed them upon his lap. For some odd reason, the bus ride home was faster than usual to her. His stop came, and he gracefully got up. As he got up she hesitantly reached her arm out touching him on his shoulder.

"Hey Covey? You can sit here anytime you want." She seemed to have softened somewhat.

"Thank you. I would like that. Enjoy the rest of your day." He turned when he got to the bus door and looked at her. He smiled brightly, and she could feel her heart continue to soften. She hoped her seat would never be empty again.

The bus rolled up to her stop and she collected her things and got off eagerly. A cool breeze blew through the air and the leaves swirled around her. She stopped and suddenly wondered where the wind would be carrying them this time.

September 30, 2008

She woke up feeling good about the day. Her classes always went smoothly. They were always filled with the popular students making stupid remarks and getting in trouble. It served as her entertainment. She liked to get through the day with as little conversation as possible. She was hoping that she would bump into Covey in school, but it never happened that way.

Today was moving particularly fast and as the bell sounded for lunch she decided to grab her calculus textbook to be proactive. She tried to always bring her own lunch because she hated waited in the long lines in the cafeteria. She grabbed a seat at the corner of the lunchroom. She liked to sit at the round tables, but it seemed that there was never enough room for her.

She took a seat and opened her textbook. She was in the mood to write so she pulled out her diary, but was sure to hide it by using her calculus book. As she started to write down her thoughts she overheard a girl say, "Covey." She looked up in the direction of the girl and started to stare. She was curious to know if the girl was talking about the same guy she knew. She watched as a girl with bouncy-curly hair get up and was followed by another student. Everyone from the table got up, but there was one girl who stayed. She hadn't even realized she was staring the entire time until the girl got out of her seat and walked towards her. She tried pretending that the girl was not now standing over her. After what seemed to be the longest few seconds of her life the girls' friends had returned. It prompted her to sit back down at her own table. Somehow she felt connected to the girl. She lowered the book and decided to mouth something to her. She wasn't sure if the girl understood, but it was worth a shot. She was just ready for three o'clock and the bus ride home.

*   *   *

"What in the world did she mouth to her?" Little Bear thought. He wondered how this girl who seems to have no friends except for Covey, could feel such a connection with some other girl. Little Bear had a feeling there was so much he was missing out on, but he read on . . .

*   *   *

November 3, 2008

Every day was a joy looking forward to three o'clock. She hadn't learned much about Covey, but his presence kept her at ease. She could feel his warmth when he finally got on the bus and sat down. They always exchanged a friendly smile, but of course his always made her get lost in a world of wonder. She mused over many things, like why he came to her, why he was so nice to her and if it was all just her imagination. She wasn't in love with him, but just the idea that someone could be so genuinely kind-hearted left her questioning things. Covey's stop came up and he started to gather his papers to get off the bus. As he began to walk down the aisle she grabbed his arm.

He turned around with a friendly confused smile and a tilt of his head.

"Um, can you get off at my stop? I would like to show you something."

He took a deep sigh and sat back down. Together they got off at 150th and started to walk. He noticed that this part of town was a trailer park lot. He tripped a few times from the uneven sidewalks and started to walk with his head down. The filthy stench surrounded him and he couldn't seem to get used to it.

He calmly asked, "Where are we going?"

Without words she continued to lead the way. She pointed to the right to let him know which home was hers. Her trailer was small. It looked like it couldn't hold more than two rooms. All the lights were out. The porch was raggedy and the railing was missing. The front yard was small, and one naked tree stood tall over the house casting an eerie shadow over the already terrible sidewalk.

Up ahead in the distance was a building where there used to be a small school. It seemed as if it had been unattended forever. Covey did not know she attended the school years ago when she was five years old. They walked around towards the back of the school. There was a huge field in the back and it oversaw the main highway in the distance and a beautiful skyline. She pulled him along into a doorway. The doorway was hidden and it was enclosed with solid brick walls all around.

She flashed back to a time as a little girl running freely in the open field. The kids had been playing kickball and she was eager to join. When she asked the other kids they pointed and laughed. The boy who wore his overalls unstrapped screamed in her face, "You know you are too fat to keep up! Just go sit and watch how it's done." At her age she had not realized that she had been bigger than most of the kids until that awful moment. She covered her face with her hands and ran over to the doorway. The kids couldn't see her. She felt safe there.

"Covey, this is where I go to get away," she stated as if he had not guessed it already.

"Oh, um . . . well this is nice," his voice was not convincing, though his curiosity was strong.

"Yes, well the reason why I bought you here is because I would love to know more about you."

"Ha! Well, I am from Portland. I am traveling across the states to see my mother. It has been a long time since I have seen her. I promised I would finish up school and do my best to understand."

"Understand what?"

"It's something I cannot explain. You just have to know. But enough about me; who are you? That's the real question."

She suddenly fell silent. He tried to peer through her dark lenses but failed. For some reason tears began to roll down her face. Covert drew near and with much confusion he asked what was wrong.

"Just get away from me! Just leave me alone," her voice was now commanding and angry, like when they first met on the bus.

"I don't understand what's wrong."

"I said . . . GET AWAY FROM ME!"

Covey looked around him to see if anybody had heard her screaming.

"Why are you doing this to me?"

"Doing what? I have done nothing. I am not going to hurt you. Please, just tell me what is wrong. What did I do?"

She fell silent again. Her heavy breathing seemed to bounce off the brick walls. She had turned away from him and was staring off into the distance. Tears continued to flow down her face. Her mouth went dry and her body was shaking miserably. She finally spoke and it threw Covert off guard. Her last words of the night would explain a lot to him.

"I don't have any friends. I always sat by myself. Then here you come acting like you could be my friend or something. Stop making fun of me. I just don't understand . . . Why are you being so nice?"

Covey looked at her in disbelief. It was at that moment he began to understand.

"Don't you believe you are worthy of that? Hasn't anyone ever told you that it would all be okay?" She was leaning against the wall and still didn't speak. "Can't you say these words; 'I am worthy?' I don't have all the time in the world to live here but in the next eight months to a year I believe it will change. I know you don't want to talk to me anymore, but I know you are listening. Everything will be okay. Tonight I challenge you to accept yourself as you are right now. There is a difference between knowing something and accepting something. You may know what you have been through, but you forgot to accept yourself. This world has probably said and done some terrible things to you. Society has probably told and made you feel as if you are not worthy. Remember these words tonight and forever. Don't let the world be the judge on how you judge the world."

Covey got straight up in her face. She seemed to glare right past him through her dark glasses. He leaned in even closer and looked her straight in the eyes and said, "I am proud of you. You do not understand now, but someday you will." He put his hand on top of her head and said, "You have been touched by an angel." She finally fell to the ground in tears. He walked away and disappeared into the cool night.

Chapter 6—The Unseen Reflection

(New York)

June 10, 2004

(Girl 2)

He was perfect for her. Everyone knew him as the coolest kid in the 8th grade. Her love story had come true. He was indeed the sweetest guy she had met. She could easily get lost in her dream world, imagining how they would walk hand in hand down the aisle until she could gracefully glaze in his eyes and passionately say "I do."

June 27, 2005

His smack across her face caught her off guard. Her blood quickly stained her well polished teeth. The numbness of her cheeks left her in shock to even speak a word, or perhaps the sting left too sharp of a pain as her tongue had been crushed instantly between her teeth. Perhaps it was the look on his face as he stood coldly over her with a smirk that made that twinkle in his eye disappear like magic.

It had been a little over a year in their relationship. She thought he would never hit her. Now, he was not all that big in size, but she could not help to feel vulnerable. All she could think was, how could something as simple as another guy looking at her get her smacked? It dumbfounded her how he could find the only spot in the mall where no one else seemed to be around.

Why can't I scream? Her thoughts seemed to scuttle together like crabs in a bucket. She kept her breathing quiet, but the motion of her chest was rapid from the rush of air in and out of her lungs. As she slowly turned her head back to the direction from which the taste had just been slapped out of her mouth, he stood with his arms open and extended towards her. He took off his hat and leaned in close.

"Now, baby do you see what happens when you piss me off. Don't be afraid. You made me do this. Put this hat on and for the rest of the time you keep your head low. Do you understand me? And if anybody asks why one side of your face is swollen what are you going to tell them?"

She thought to herself . . . could this really be a question he dared to ask? He moved in even closer. He was smooth as he used his thumb and pointer finger to clasp her chin and slowly lift her head up towards him.

"You are going to tell them that you just came from the dentist. That's all they need to know. Now, just be a good little girlfriend and let's enjoy the rest of the day. Anyway, Foot Locker's having a sale. You know you said you were gonna get me some shoes."

Enjoy the rest of the day . . . . As if. But she robotically shook her head in compliance. Besides it was not all that bad; maybe she was being overly dramatic. After all, the swelling had already begun to cease. She figured she would never have to speak the truth of this to anyone. Everyone gets a second chance, right? Maybe it was her fault . . . she could be a little high maintenance sometimes.

They began to walk again. This time the pace was not as enthusiastic. As she walked she counted each square she walked over. The squares on the floor were in an interesting pattern. Two squares were side by side with perfect coordinating colors; a black and white combo. Then a few feet apart from those squares would be a single square. It seemed as if it had drifted away from the coordinating pair. It was probably misunderstood. There was no color to it, only an outline with a clear center, as if someone forgot to make it black or white. She wondered if anybody had even noticed this square. She wondered if anybody had even noticed her. A total of ten empty squares she had counted.

August 30, 2005

Of course it didn't feel good, but it was the one thing that took the pain away from all the other things that went wrong. The beatings had continued and only gotten worse. She couldn't leave him though. Who could love him like she did? She feared for him more than herself. She looked at the razor and nodded her head. This had to be done. She had been lying in the tub fully clothed with her sleeves rolled all the way up. The blood slithered towards her fingers and each drip rolled off her fingertips into the tub inching towards the drain slowly. She reached for the small white face towel and gently dabbed at the cuts that now ran down her arms like railroad tracks through an abandoned town. The blood quickly stained the cloth, and it gave her a queasy feeling to go with the strange relief she got from slitting open her own skin with a razor.

A gentle knock came on the bathroom door. Her clueless mother had always knocked three times anytime there was a closed door: one for respect, two for warning, and three for response. If someone would take too long to respond she would come in. The third knock ended and the door knob began to twist.

"Wait, don't come in. I'm changing."

"Young lady hurry up in there. It's been thirty minutes. We are late and your grandmother isn't getting any younger."

She rolled her eyes, and quickly stashed away her blood stained cloth along with the razor in the usual secret spot behind the box in the vanity cabinet. She wiped out the bathtub carefully. It was much easier than the tile floor when it came to erasing blood. She walked out of the bathroom and into her room to apply her makeup. While putting on her lip gloss her phone rang. The caller ID read in big bold letters MY EVERYTHING. She knew if the phone would get to a fifth ring without her answering it he would be pissed. She scrambled to the bed and picked up the phone.

"What took you so long," her boyfriend Mal's voice on the other end was brutal and cold.

"I was getting ready to go to the hospital to see my grandma."

"Whatever . . . Don't keep me waiting next time. What time you are coming back?"

"I'm not sure. You know we have to drive all the way upstate."

"You not trying to avoid me are you," he managed to sound crushed by this somehow. "I miss you baby. I want to take you out, and make up for my behavior. Come on baby cakes . . . stay behind and tell your mom you got other plans. Your grandma will be fine. What do you say? You know the right answer, right baby?"

With him there was never really a correct answer. But she knew the only expected answer for anything he asked was yes. Her head was spinning. At her door came three knocks. Not even two seconds later her mother walked in. The girl sat in the corner of her bed with the phone tightly clenched in her hands. Her mother crossed her arms and raised her eyebrow.

"This is not the time for love games." Her mother said through clenched teeth as she darted to the bed and snatched the phone out of her hands. "She's gonna have to call you back." She hung up the phone and dragged her down the stairs. Together her, her mother and brother headed upstate to see her grandma.

All she could think about was how much trouble she was going to be in when she came back home and would have to see him again. She stared out the car window hopelessly. She rubbed her cheeks in circles over and over again, hoping the sensation would distract her from the pain she was feeling inside. She could already feel the slap she was going to receive from him. Perhaps someone else was feeling worse pain, she thought trying to gather herself.

*   *   *

How could someone else know all of this? Little Bear was more sure than ever of two things now. First, that girl whose letter he read before really was his sister. It didn't just seem like her, it really <u>was</u> her. Second, he knew that somehow, whoever wrote the typewritten pages in the envelope knew all of them. He was reading about an actual day in the life of his own family. He thought he had understood that day, but apparently he knew only a little. Seeing what his sister was going through had more than driven that point home. Who knew them like this?? The typed pages continued, and of course, the story held Little Bear's rapt attention. He tried to close his mouth to mask his shock as he read more about his sister's no-longer-secret nightmare of a life.

*   *   *

January 10, 2006

A new year had come quickly, but painfully. By this time she had been with him for almost two years. Some things had remained the same and other things became worse. Over time his hits had become more powerful. He refrained from the slaps to the face more these days because he was running out of fabrications to cover up for the bruises and contusions they caused. Instead his punches went directly to her stomach. Knocking the wind out of her guts kept her from talking and screaming more anyway. He always promised he would change and she wanted nothing more than to hold him to that. And he was clearly trying. He was always so nice to her after he hurt her. He must love her if he was doing that, right? But everything started to become very hard to cope with for her. Her father was pretty much out of her life now, her appetite had long ago ceased, and as if things couldn't get worse, her grandmother had not gotten much better. The treatment had stopped working. Nana's cancer was continuing to spread.

She sat up in her bed drying her tears. It was one in the morning. She decided to head down to the kitchen to find something she could bear to eat. As she made it to the kitchen she noticed the fridge door was open. She stopped in her tracks. She was swept with an overwhelming fear as she flashed back to a time when her boyfriend was searching through his fridge after he had just got done beating her up. He punched her twice in the stomach and made her apologize for causing his outburst by startling him. She remembered standing in the hall looking into the kitchen at him and as he closed the door he smiled and said, "Are you satisfied now?" The sudden vision had sent chills through her body.

She snapped out of her distressing reverie when her brother touched her on the shoulder. "What's wrong with you," her brother's voice came in a fearful tone. "I've been calling your name for like two minutes."

"Nothing I was only thinking."

"It's about Nana, right? I'm scared, sis."

"It's okay Little Bear she is going to make it." She wished her spoken hopes could bring their grandmother the kind of relief they all needed in some way. Come on now get the milk out so we can head back to bed and I'll get the crackers. We have to be up early to head upstate to see her."

"Okay," her little brother smiled at ease as she tussled with his hair. As he sat the milk on the counter he heard her moan in pain. "What's wrong sis?"

"Nothing my stomach just hurts a little bit."

"Oh okay. Is it like when mommy tells us not to bother her because her tummy hurts?"

"Yes, let's go with that. Now time for ten year old boys to march upstairs and sleep."

"Okay, fine. You know what I think? I think you're nervous. But don't be so nervous. Mr. Chiphaliwali always tells us life is a performance. You are on a stage. You don't always know your audience, but you know all the lines. I like him a lot. If you nervous it's okay. The show will go on.

"Awe Little Bear I'll keep that in mind. Now, move it."

January 28, 2006

She and her brother were waiting down in the lobby of the hospital for their mother to return, and then it would be her turn to see her Nana. Her brother got up from his seat and went over to the small wishing fountain.

He called out, "Sis, you gotta see this. It's gotta be a million pennies in here. Can I please have some pennies? I wanna make a wish."

She shook her head in laughter, "Little Bear that's just a way for them to steal your money." She got up from her seat and started to walk across the lobby to the fountain. Out the corner of her eye she spotted a shiny penny. Perfect, she thought. As she went down to pick it up she looked at the tiles on the floor. There was an outline of a square but it was simply blank on the inside. All the other squares had some type of intricate design in them. Weird, she thought. She reached her brother. By then she realized she had counted a total of ten empty squares.

"What took so long, gee? Mr. Chiphaliwali always tells us the gift of life can come from the simplest of wishes. So, gimme ten pennies. One for every year. That way the wish has to come true."

"Why not just a dime then?"

"Earth to big-head," he said clasping his hands over his mouth to make the static noise of a radio "this is a penny fountain it only works with pennies. Oh my God. Come on sis, *Are You Smarter Than a Fifth Grader?*"

She smacked him on the back of his head. "You deserved that, and the only one I have is this penny." He snatched the penny out of her hand and closed his eyes. His bottom lip moved slightly while he wished to himself.

"Well, what did you wish Little Bear?" Right as he was about to speak he pointed across to the other side of the lobby towards their mother. "Okay . . . hold on to that thought. After I see Nana then you can tell me."

*   *   *

Little Bear laughed to himself as he remembered that moment. Then he laughed at himself, realizing that it so happened he was jingling his spare change in his pocket with his free hand while he read. He had always saved pennies there, since that day, in case another opportunity for a wish came up. He hadn't let himself think about that habit of his for a long time. But even though it had been 6 years ago, that morning at the hospital fountain, he certainly remembered the wish he made . . . .

*   *   *

She headed onto the elevator and pressed the button to the third floor. The elevator music played somberly in the background. The doors opened on the second floor and a young girl who could not have been older than five walked onto the elevator with a balloon tied to her wrist that read get well soon. Her brown hair reached evenly to her neck and a red bow was tied perfectly in her hair. Her dress was a flawless white color and matched her shoes.

She looked curiously at the girl and pointed to the arrow and said, "Sweetie this elevator is going up."

"I know. I am going up to see Him."

The elevator beeped as it reached the third floor and the doors slowly opened. She waited to see if the little girl was getting off too, but she didn't budge. She walked off the elevator and looked back at the girl. The little girl smiled and waved goodbye. *She never even pushed a button.* She half smiled back and walked down the hall to Room 303. She slowly opened the door to the room and walked in.

"Nana," she whispered softly, but with the stillness of the room it sounded more like a shout.

"Come here honey," her grandmother's voice was peaceful. She went up to her side. She observed that the I.V. was on the top of her hand coiled around her arm. There were several machines that beeped a constant discordant tune. She grabbed the hand of her grandmother. Her hands had a tough appearance, but were soft to the touch. She looked at her face and followed the wrinkles that seem to weave in and out of each other. They made an articulate design that traveled to the creases of her cheeks which made it look as if she were always smiling. Her hair was left in patches but combed back wherever possible. The lump inside her head from the tumor had grown into the size of a ripe cherry.

"Don't worry honey," her grandmother said breaking the silence, "it doesn't hurt as bad as it looks."

"Oh Nana," she said as her vision became blurry from the tears.

"I know, but listen I am very happy. I get to join Pa in heaven now. You need to set yourself free. You're just like your mother; always worrying about the wrong things. Keep your faith my child." Her grandmother began to touch her face using her soft hands to stroke her granddaughter's smooth cheeks. "You are so beautiful, and you have to believe in that. If you get caught up in the wrong things it makes you ugly. Your character is determined by your actions not your looks, and my child believe in me when I tell you; that beauty is skin deep and ugly is to the bone. If you ever need me you'll know just where to look. I must get my rest now."

"Yes Nana." She was staring at the ground. She realized she had been standing in one of those empty squares. She swung her head back up and hugged her Nana with all she had. She headed towards the door and looked back. "I love you Nana."

"I love you more."

She closed the door and then fell to the floor in tears. Her phone vibrated in her pocket. It read one missed call from MY EVERYTHING.

February 6, 2006

One ring. No answer. Two rings. No answer. Three rings. No answer.

"Hello,"

"Finally you answer. Come out now I am ready to leave."

"I told you I can't today we are going to see Nana."

"She's still alive? Well I am not asking you. I am telling you that you coming out with me today. You don't wanna hurt my feelings do you?"

"No, I am sorry. I'll tell my mom I gotta finish something for school tomorrow."

"Hurry up, K? bye."

She hung up the phone and went to tell her mother. She didn't want to see him today, but maybe today he would be like his real self, from before . . . . That sweet guy she once met. Or maybe not. She dragged her feet slowly downstairs contemplating the story she would use to get out of going today. Her words came out in a rush.

"Mom I can't make it today I have to finish a project for school."

"Honey can't it wait. I'll write you a note or something this is important to your grandmother."

"Um, no. He said no exceptions. I'll go this weekend. I don't wanna be too tired for school."

"Okay baby." She reached over and gave her daughter a kiss on the forehead. "Just make sure you don't stay up too late, and lock the door in the morning when you leave for school because we're just going to stay the night instead."

"Okay." She watched her family load up in the car and pull off. Not even five seconds later there was a knock on the back door. She ran quickly to the door and opened it. Without words he pointed to her and moved his fingers inward towards him. She nodded her head and asked him to wait one minute. She went back got her clothes for the next day and made sure all the doors were locked. She would just spend the night at his house and be sure to go straight home after school.

She got in the car. "What took so long for you to come? Damn do us both a favor and try not to piss me off tonight."

"Sorry I had to lock the doors. Where are we going?"

Can you shut the hell up and let me drive?" She closed her mouth and just looked out the window. She saw the little neighborhood girls Brenda, Brianna, and Olivia playing hopscotch. Ten perfect squares come together to make the game, but life is no game, she thought. She envisioned herself being able to play the game with the girls. She would throw her rock in order to skip over the fourth square. She hated that number. If she could skip it, things would be perfect. Then daddy couldn't leave mommy. Her thoughts drifted away as the young girls waved at her. She smiled her best fake smile, trying to pass for happy as the car finally passed them and turned the corner.

February 7, 2006

The car pulled up in front of the house. "Get out of my car now! I am tired of seeing your face. Next time you don't wake me up for school, I am *really* gonna teach you a lesson.

"Alright," the attitude in her voice was too obvious. As she reached out for the door handle her neck was yanked back. He grabbed a fist full of her hair and pulled her head so close she felt like he was breathing her air.

"Drop your attitude it turns me off," he whispered in a low growl. He unbuckled his seat belt and opened her door. He took his left leg and lifted it kicking her in her back and out of the car. He drove away quickly and rounded the corner. She got up off the sidewalk wiping her eyes.

When she got to the door it was still locked. Her phone was dead so she couldn't call her mom. She sat on the steps and waited for almost two hours before her mom finally pulled up in the drive way. Her mother quickly got out the car and unlocked the door. She never even acknowledged her daughter. Her brother followed out of the car dragging his feet slowly towards the door.

"Little Bear what's wrong?" The look he gave her was the same look she had once given her dad when he left; a look of total disappointment.

"Nana didn't make it," he yelled in sorrow.

"What are you talking about? Don't joke like that."

He brushed her off his shoulders. "You should have been there, but instead you lied. I'm your brother I know when you lying to mom. Nana cried for you. I hate you so much for not being there. You ruined my only wish." Her brother ran into the house slamming the door behind him.

She dropped to the ground crying uncontrollably. *Nana, I'm sorry I failed you. I'm sorry I wasn't there. I'll never be worthy enough now. Please forgive me.* A cold breeze blew. Small snowflakes began to hit the ground. Change was in the air.

*   *   *

Little Bear wiped away the tears that were now obscuring his vision. He couldn't just read on like this. He didn't even know who he felt the most sadness for, even this many years later. It almost hurt to know how much more than he realized had happened that day . . . .

*   *   *

CHAPTER 7—Little Things Big Surprises

(Midlothian, IL)

March 24, 2006

(Girl 3)

This was the moment of truth. Her baby was about to be born. The bright lights of the hospital room sent her into a frenzy of thoughts. The voices repeatedly reminded her to take a deep breath and try to relax. She had never felt such physical pain before. She begged the doctors to please give her something to stop the intense pain.

"Concentrate on your breathing and think of something else besides the pain," said the man in white as his latex gloves snapped onto his hands. She wondered if he thought he was being helpful.

At that moment the room turned black. She flashed back in time almost nine months ago to the day the baby was conceived in June. She remembered everything that happened as she let her mind slide into the bright hospital lights that were shining in her eyes . . . .

June 2, 2005

"I promise I will take care of you. You have to trust me and if I hurt you I promise I will stop." His tone was smooth and convincing.

"Okay but I'm still nervous."

He kissed her soft lips and began to strip her of her clothing. She knew what she was doing was wrong. Her parents did not even trust her and if they found out she snuck some guy into the house they would kill her. His hands started to explore her legs and thighs. Her heavy breathing became more apparent the closer he got to her.

"No this is a bad idea," she whispered, "I can't do this, I'm not ready."

"It's fine if you just relax it will feel good, alright. Trust me I know these things."

She just laid there with her head facing up looking towards the ceiling. She never cried. As she lied there in shock she wondered what price she would have to pay for this. He got up not too long after and got his things.

"It's not so bad after awhile," he said as he reached for the door, "you just have to learn how to relax."

The door crept closed behind him.

August 30, 2005

The battle at home with her parents became intense.

"All we are saying is that we have noticed a mood swing in you. We are tired of you giving us an attitude. This is our house and if you don't like the rules then it is what it is." The only reason her mother was speaking like this was because her father had threatened her to get tougher on the kids.

"See," her father's voice cut in, "you are not listening, and that's your problem. No child is going to disrespect me. All this staying out late ends today. Only the good Lord knows what you're doing on the streets."

"Hun, don't yell at her. Look you know if you have something to tell us you absolutely can. We love you, and we are here for you."

As she shook her head she thought to herself that her parents would never understand and that she would never tell them anything. She gave a small smile to reassure them she was fine and hurried off back to her room. She picked up the phone and called her friend. She needed advice on her stomach pains. She had been hiding it in hopes things would work out, but she had missed her period. The phone call was brief and ended only with the advice that she should take a home pregnancy test. It was not the advice she was hoping for. How was she supposed to go about this?

She left to the pharmacy to buy a home test. As she entered the store she felt the whole store was watching her. She found just the aisle for what she needed. She danced around the boxes trying to be as inconspicuous as possible. She observed a lady, who looked to be in her twenties, pick up one of the tests. She flipped the box around and read each word, then mumbled something and took the box and headed to the register. She mimicked what the lady did and dashed towards the register. As she took each step closer to her turn she looked around, feeling conspicuous, careful to be sure no one she knew spotted her. As she was finally next in line she placed a pack of gum, a Twix, and the test on the counter. She had already run over the lie in her head what she would say if she cashier asked why she was purchasing a pregnancy test. *You see it's for my friend. She is too shy to come in and get it herself. Besides I am too young for the stuff anyway. Wouldn't you agree? And does this Twix come in peanut butter?* The cashier began to ring up the items and she turned her focus to a newspaper headline that read: PLANE CRASH LEAVES LITTLE HOPE! She sure knew all about having little hope.

"Hello, young lady," an impatient voice rang out, "I asked is that all for you today."

"Oh sorry, yes it is." She tossed a few bills on the counter and said keep the change as she headed out of the sliding doors.

She made it home and darted up into the bathroom. She locked the door and took the test.

September 12, 2005

Her belly had started to become tight and round. She had lost the motivation for most things. The worst part was she still had not told her parents. The days were becoming a drag and school was starting to take its toll. She walked in her house one day after school and her parents had been waiting in the living room for her.

"Get in here now!" Her father's voice was demanding.

She closed the door and dropped her things. Her heart was pounding rapidly. She took a deep breath and put on a straight face as she entered the living room.

"Yes."

"Have a seat."

She decided to sit as close to the door as possible . . . just in case.

"Tell us something," he started to say as he inched forward in his chair with a puzzled look on his face and one finger strongly pointing at her, "how is it you failing classes already and that your teachers are concerned with your health."

She wasn't too sure how to respond to this so she slightly shrugged her shoulders.

"I am so sick and tired of you not knowing anything. So, since you don't know things anymore know this; you will not be leaving this house anymore and you will not be doing anything. From now on its school and back in this house."

"You can't keep me trapped in this house. God, you guys don't understand anything. This is really hard for me. I hate this!"

"Oh I'm sorry. I forgot how hard it is to be a kid, and to do whatever I want to. You think you have it so hard?"

"Now hold on a second," her mother's voice began to intervene, "maybe there is something difficult for her. I mean maybe we are being too tough on her."

"Are you kidding me? All she does in this house is eat and sleep. She is getting fat, she doesn't help out around the house, she failing in school and God knows what she is doing out on the streets."

She stood up from the chair. Her eyes were flooded with tears and she hadn't even realized it yet. "I don't have to take this. I am leaving."

"Hun please"—but her mother's plea was cut off.

"Let her go. She will be back when she's good and ready. I am tired of the disrespect."

The door closed and she headed off on her own. She was unsure of what to do or where to go. All she thought about was her so-called boyfriend. How was he going to take the news to know he was to be a father?

March 24, 2006

The flashback had taken her mind off the birth long enough to find out it was finally over. The nurses had returned from weighing the baby.

The baby girl was swaddled, wrapped up in cocoon style in the soft white blankets.

"Here is your beautiful healthy girl."

"Hello Lillian. I am your mommy." The baby's crying ceased. She rocked Lillian slowly and watched her eyes close wearily. She whispered gently in her ear. "I promise with all my soul I will do anything to protect you from this cold world. Mommy is going to love you forever."

One of the nurses took Lillian to the nursery with the rest of the new born children.

"Excuse me nurse, what is your name?"

"My name is Ms. Love. Sweetie you have had a long day. We are going to contact your parents, and let them know that you are okay."

"NO! Please! You can't do that. My parents don't know about any of this."

"Oh my God," Ms. Love started at her bedside, "Well, I feel that you should be the one to tell them, but where in the world do they think you are?"

She could feel her blood pressure rising. The thumping in her temple began to beat like African drums. Her voice went hoarse and tears seem to stream from every part of her eyes. Ms. Love shut the hospital room door and went back to her side.

"I have been raped and I lied about it. My boyfriend raped me and got me pregnant," she was quivering as she took a deep breath, "My father was getting on my nerves, I swear I wanted to tell them, but then I ran away to a friend's house, and I just don't know what to do!"

Ms. Love sat by her bed staring off, dumbfounded. She reminisced to a time when her own daughter had run away. It had almost been eight years since she had seen her. She could still remember their last goodbye before sending her off to Portland to her Aunt's house for her daughter's own safety. She promised herself that if she could prevent someone else such pain from not having a relationship with their child she would. Ms. Love was all too familiar from running away from her own problems. She had come to Illinois in order to escape her own crooked path where she had been abused. Sitting there looking at her cry in that bed from all the pain and confusion, Ms. Love knew exactly what she must do.

"I can help sweetie," the sound of her voice startled both of them. "Let me take care of Lillian and when you are ready you can take her back at anytime. This will help so when you finally have the courage to tell your parents, you'll know where to find her."

"I don't understand. Why would you take care of her?"

"Because I know what it feels like to be alone and scared. And I know what it's like not to be able to find your child when you have the strength to take care of them. I have not seen my daughter in years, because I was afraid to take a stand, but I decided someday I would have the courage, and now that I have it, I want to give you that same option."

"What if I never gain the courage? I want Lillian, but I can't bring her into my world at this point in my life."

"I'll adopt her, but it will be for you. You can come at any time and see her. We don't have to tell your daughter anything you are not ready for her to know about you. Look, it has been a long night. Why don't you sleep on it and I'll get all the paper work together and in the morning you can decide what you would like to do."

"Okay, but what about my parents?'

"Rest, sweetheart. They have gone this long worrying about you without knowing exactly where you are. I don't think one more night will kill them."

CHAPTER 8—One Final Step

(Portland, Oregon)

April 10, 2009

(Girl 4)

Dear Serenity,

What do you fear the most? You have had some circumstances in your life that have changed your perspective about many things. As a person you capture my heart. Perhaps your love is one of the purest loves I can recall. I asked you a few weeks back "why you" and I did not ask you this question to confuse you with all your troubles and heartache. The old adage goes, "Everything happens for a reason." The things you have shared with me do not tell me why these things have happened to you, but rather they tell me a story of how things came to be. So, now I ask you, what do you fear the most? Do your fears consist of being alone with no one to love? So, once again I ask you, "Why you?" and I also ask you, "What do you fear?"

Is it not serendipitous how we met? You stumbled upon me by reading the newspaper article from years ago, about the plane crash that took the life of my mother, clearly a huge misfortunate that took place in my life. So, I ask again—why you? I feel it is comical we all have this perception about how different we all are. We think our styles, language, food, and religious beliefs separate us, but in the end, these things truly link us closer together. The only difference is we have each been hoodwinked into thinking that our view is the only way. Do not become blinded by your circumstances. Your struggle is tough to cope with, but pity on someone else is not the reason we should all come together. The universal feeling we have all felt is pain, and there is no feeling worse than being alone while feeling such intense pain. Know that my love for you does not come from pity, but rather from empathy because I too know the pain all too well myself. The only way to conquer the pain of humanity is not to run, but to find peace in those who have conquered pain through love. So, what do you fear the most, and why you?

Agape,
Covey

April 30, 2009

Dear Covey,

I am not sure what I fear the most. I feel alone right now. I am wearing my ring praying things will get better. I hate how every boy I have ever dated just uses me. I really do my best to be perfect for them. I do not know what to do anymore. I want to run away again so bad right now. You just keep asking me these questions that I don't understand. Covey, when will I see you? Can you please just take me away from this house, this place, this life? I know you don't have it perfect, but why does it feel like everybody but me does? I am tired of pain, Covey. I want nothing more than just to be happy for once. I don't think God likes me very much.

I feel like the world is watching me, but instead of reassuring me, it is pointing its finger at me and laughing whole-heartedly. I feel so empty. I think my biggest fear is simply that this emptiness will never subside. I think about my father every day. I think about my mother every day, too. Covey, she is long gone. She moved me here and left. How can you tell ME not to run when that is what she has been doing her entire life? I will never see her again and there is no telling when I will see my father. I still see myself as that little girl who watched all these terrible things unfold. I will never grow old and see joy, because pain is all I know. I am watching my life pass me by. Please, Covey, help me get through this. I think you are the only source of peace I have left.

I Love You,
Serenity

May 4, 2009

Dear Serenity,

If you are reading this then you should be proud of yourself. You did not run away. Deep down inside you are tired of running. I am honored you have found peace in me. Great things do come for those who wait. I can only imagine how many times you have read over my letters or thought about the phone calls. When great things come our way we check for the path it leaves behind to make sure it's real. But you don't always need to know what's behind you. Be where you are. Go into the places that you deserve. Take up your rightful space. The best part is you'll never have to speak of greatness because it will show. Serenity, you are great, now. I say this proudly because despite all the heartache that you have claimed you have put your last bit of sanity into, something you feel is real, and now you are living for that.

One day, and I am not sure as to when, but you will be united with your mother, just as I will be united with my own. There is no doubt in my mind that she thinks about you every day. You may feel at this point that you are that little girl just continually watching the entirety of the pain unfold in front of you, but imagine how your mother must feel? She only remembers you as her little innocent angel, who she had to sacrifice to save you from so much more suffering and grief. She has not yet gained the strength to come back into your life. Forgive her, for she is afraid that you will not let her back in. She is looking for her hidden peace to give her the strength she needs to reunite with you. God is still watching over you. He will always love you. And you and I will meet one day. I promise you that.

Did you know that my biggest fear is not being able to do anything about the circumstances in which I was chosen to live? Why was I chosen for this life? Well, attitude goes a long way. If you want things to change you first have to change your mind set. I believe in you like never before. What steps are you willing to take to change your life around? This is your moment. You are not a reflection of things that happened to you; you are a reflection of things that can change. Always remember that people don't change; circumstances do, and how we respond to those changes create our character and who we are. We can always infer the how, but to understand the why we must be willing to accept the things we cannot change.

With Agape,
Covey

May 19, 2009

Dear Covey,

How am I ever supposed to thank you enough? Your words have guided me to an understanding I would have never reached on my own accord. I am switching my focus for the better. I have decided that I can do this. Everything does happen for a reason and I really don't know why all the time, but that's ok, because it has still bettered me. Covey, can you believe I finally found a sweet boy who makes me happy? He is there when I need him and has been my reassurance and guidance. I am happier than I can ever recall.

Guess what? I even heard from my mother. She said she is going to be coming back home in time for my graduation in 2012. She said no one could ever replace me and that she thought about me every day, just like you told me. Covey, can you please come to my graduation, too? It would be perfect. I would have my mother back and the one person who stuck it out with me the entire time.

Look . . . I have no idea whom or what you are, but because of you I am setting myself free. I am taking the final step on my own. I hope we will see each other in 2012. Please know I will always carry your words with me. You are the light that has shined on me along the entire way, and now with my new found faith I will not be afraid to walk head first into the darkness. I love you, and I will never be sure or not if you were just a piece of my imagination, but you have taught me that impossible is nothing more than a limitation of the imagination, and I will never again be afraid to explore the beautiful life that I now know that I have.

My Freedom,
Serenity Love

CHAPTER 9—The Leaf

(Harvey, IL)

November 3, 2008

(Girl 1)

She sat crying in her secret doorway spot at the school, right where he had just left. Her body had this unfamiliar rush of emotion passing through her. The cool air made her tears feel like icicles dripping slowly to the sides of her face. She had barely mustered enough courage to stand back up on her feet in the spot from which she had fallen. She slowly started her walk into the darkness back home. All of Covey's words whistled more loudly then the wind blowing in her face.

Could he really be proud of me? He called himself an angel. All this time searching for someone to love me and now this guy gives me all the hope in the world.

She made it back to the trailer and rushed to her room to write down the mind-boggling events that had just occurred. She didn't even notice the smell of the trash that lined the alleys along her way back. The only thing in her mind was the conversation she had just had.

November 4, 2008

At three o'clock she waited eagerly for Covey to take his seat on the bus. She wasn't sure what she was to say to him, but just seeing him would soothe the uneasy feeling and all the thoughts that cluttered her head. He never came. She began to miss his luminous smile. She thought she could hear his voice clearly in her head. *But maybe it was all one big dream. There is no such person named Covey.* The bus rolled on without him. As she stood up to get off the bus she took a peak down the bus aisle in hopes that he was in the very back and just hadn't seen him. He wasn't there.

November 5, 2008

Three o'clock had taken too long to come. The celebration throughout the nation had begun. School was filled with excited students screaming YES WE DID. The excitement had come from announcement that the winner of the election, and therefore new President-Elect was Barack Obama. The bus had come thirty minutes later than usual due to the traffic that had swamped the streets. In the normative chaos of getting on the bus she noticed someone in her seat. As she drew closer she could feel his presence.

"Covey, where were you yesterday?"

"I stayed after yesterday. Hey, how excited are you about Obama winning? I have a good feeling that things will change."

"Um, sure." She was trying to hide her frustration, but the truth was she had missed him. She wondered how could he sit there and not think about the message he had given her the other day. She took her seat. *At least he is real?*

"Covey, are going to be getting off at my stop?"

"Yes, I can do that for you."

Together the two of them begin to take the voyage back to the secret doorway. When they reached the doorway she sat down.

"So . . . anything that you would like to discuss?" Covert asked, breaking the awkward silence.

"Covey. I have been thinking. I cannot thank you enough for caring for me so much and becoming a great friend, but I want to feel beautiful, and not need someone to tell it to me all the time. Plus, I am tired of people staring at me and snickering behind my back like I don't hear them."

"I understand."

"No! That's the thing. No you don't. I was walking through the hallways the other day and two guys behind me were making rude noises for every step I took. I know it was directed at me because when I stopped and turned around they were looking down at my feet laughing. Then they just ran off," She was starting to cry, but she used her black scarf to quickly dry the tears. She was looking down at the ground. It was too intimidating for her to look him in the eyes. "But then I get to my locker and the girl next to me stood behind tapping her feet. When I finally got my things I heard her say that waiting behind me was like being stuck behind a truck. Do you have any idea how demoralizing that is?"

"Well, please tell me what you think I can do to help you with all of this."

"I want to lose some weight, but I know I cannot do it by myself."

"Alright, tell you what. You and I will come up with a new diet and workout plan for you. It will not be easy, but I think we can do this. All I can say is be prepared by Saturday."

Covey left her seated. She wasn't sure if he was serious or not, but one thing she was sure about was that she was tired of being everyone's big joke.

November 8, 2008

Bang! Bang! Bang!

"Alright I am coming," she shouted behind the door, face scrunched up in sleep. "Covey, it's eight in the morning, what are you doing here?"

He was wearing black sweat pants, a hoodie, and a black winter cap. He was jogging in place at the doorway trying to stop the bitter cold from taking over.

"You told me you wanted my help, so here I am. Now go put on some sweats. We have some work to do."

"Why are you making fun of me? I thought you weren't like the others!"

"What are you talking about? You said you wanted my help. Now come on we don't have much time."

"I can't, Covey."

"Yes you can. Now let's do this thing."

"No, I mean I can't run, literally. What if someone sees me? They will laugh."

"It is okay. Look . . . I am going to stick by your side. You don't have to run as long as we are moving. And don't worry about other people so much because you are out here doing what you have to do, so why worry? They are not you. You are taking the steps to better yourself. If anything they will respect you."

She silently shook her head incredulously and went to change. She invited him in. When he walked into the trailer he felt as if his head was going to hit the ceiling. As she disappeared into the back to her room Covert looked around at the surroundings. The television sat in the corner on the floor. In front of the TV was an old grubby looking couch. Its plaid colors of red and black had faded into shades of dingy gray. The trailer was completed with a homey touch of family and (mostly embarrassing) baby pictures.

She returned after a few moments with an old gray sweat outfit. She had tied her hair up in a bun. What caught his attention was that she was wearing a pair of Chuck's. The old-school Converse shoes had been tied tightly past her ankles. There was not a spot of white on the old shoes.

"These are the only shoes I have!" she exclaimed defensively.

"I didn't say anything," Covert protested with his hands up in the "stop" position. Together they headed out the door towards the old abandoned school.

"Okay," Covey started, "Everyday we are going to come here. The first thing that we are always going to do is stretch. Then after we are done stretching we are going to keep moving around this school a total of four times. This should almost be equivalent to a mile if not more. Then when we are done running our mile we will stretch again. When you get home it is up to you to watch the food you eat. Then at night, right before you get into bed, you must do fifty sit-ups. I can promise you if you keep this up you will start to see results, regardless of that look on your face right now. Okay, any questions?"

She quietly shook her head no, and tried not to smile at his witty remark.

"Alright, good. First, you see this field in front of us? Well, this field will be your own field of dreams. Now, look up at the sky. The sky will represent the endless possibilities of your dreams. During the next few months I want you to dream of being a beautiful soul and then know that there is no limit to it. Stretch your arms all the way to the sky. If you feel a tug in your stomach that's a good thing, don't worry. Try taking a deep breath and clearing all those stale cells out of your system. Now, take a deep breath, hold it . . . and slowly exhale, and then we will start a light jog."

He jogged in front of her with his back facing the wind so that he was facing her. He ran backwards himself in order to encourage her while running. At first she started off mostly by walking. She fixed her eyes to Covey's eyes and her breathing became more intense. She seemed to become more determined with each step she took. Her thoughts of all the pain her body had brought on to her from others began to swarm her mind.

Hey hey hey, it's Fat Albert . . . look out its King Kong's wife . . . you can't even keep up with us . . . watch out for the big girls . . . waiting behind her is like waiting behind a truck . . . I won the bet, so give me my $5—I danced with that big girl . . . don't feed the animals!

She became swept up with emotion and for each ridiculing remark that entered her mind she took faster and harder steps around the school. Covey increased his own pace as she actually began to run. He nearly tripped over himself when she mumbled something that caught him off guard.

"I am worthy," she seemed to have whispered to herself in a panting breath. Covey was not sure he could believe his ears as the rounded the school for the last time. But she kept running and repeating the phrase to herself, whatever it was. As they came to the home stretch and finally stopped both of them were taking deep breaths.

"I am so proud of you," Covey cheered despite his own growing exhaustion. He was not about to let her know he was tired. "Now, go ahead and stretch up to the sky." She lifted her arms as high as her tired body would allow her. "Hey, listen. I know there was a lot of wind in my ears as we ran, but did you by any chance say something while we were running?"

She slowly placed her arms back to her side and winced in pain, "No, I didn't say anything."

"Oh, okay. Just checking. Well, very good job today. You are free to go and tomorrow be ready again. On the weekends we will run early in the mornings and on the weekdays we will run at five during the evening. See you tomorrow."

Even though she was ready for him to go, for once, she hated the way Covey always seemed to disappear from her at will. She headed back home. The first thing she was going to do when she returned was get out of those shoes that made her ankles and feet throb.

November 27, 2008

Most of the month continued in the same routine. She had not yet seen the results she was longing for, but Covey kept her at ease. Today was going to be different than usual. It was Thanksgiving and her father had made plans to come spend the holiday with them this year. She was in her room lying on her bed when her father came in.

"How's my number one daughter doing?"

"I'm you're only daughter, and just fine."

"You don't have to be such a smart ass. Look, kid, I don't like it either, but I am your father. You think I like coming here and watching you pathetically mope around."

"Then stop coming! Just get out of my life please."

"See there you go again. And to think I tried to come in here sober just for you. Don't you see that I'm trying?"

"You don't care and you never did!"

"You know what, why do I even bother with you? Are you listening to me? And stop writing in that damn book for one second!" He snatched her diary from her hands and flung it across the room.

She screamed out, "Why did you do that?"

"Because I can. Now pick it up. Oh, and by the way I'm taking back that Winnie the Pooh doll. I'm giving it to this new chick I'm with. She likes this yellow bear crap, and she agrees with me that you're too damn old for it anyway."

He picked up the now loosely stuffed animal and headed towards the door. She got up and gunned towards the door blocking the doorway.

"You cannot take that!"

He smacked her across the face and went out the door. He left the trailer and got into his car. She got up from the floor and grabbed her Chuck's and headed out the door. She started her laps around the school without stretching. She didn't even realize how cold it was as she rounded the school. Her breath could be seen in a full cloud as she muttered the phrase with each step. After four laps she passed out in the doorway. The wind blew so hard it picked up a pile of leaves making them dance in circles by her feet. One leaf gently swayed into her lap. She held it in her palm. She closed her eyes. *Please let the wind blow me in a new direction.* When she opened her eyes the leaf was off in the distance bouncing in the air. She smiled faintly and headed back home. When she reached her home, Covey was standing under the eerie bare tree near her broken down white gate. She ran up to him without a word and hugged him.

"Happy Thanksgiving," he said. She cried in his arms instantly. "It's okay I know you had a bad day." He hugged her tighter and coolly whispered, "Do you feel that . . . that is what agape love feels like. Remember this moment forever."

His words were so soothing and coaxing she could feel her heart melt. He walked her up to her door and then headed back out towards the raggedy white fence. He stopped and looked back at her and smiled his brilliant smile. As she saw his smile, it almost took her breath away. She looked up to the sky and saw a leaf was slowly dancing down to the ground next to

Covey. As he turned and began his walk into the cool night the leaf was swayed by his movement and started its voyage towards a new promise.

May 24, 2009

After nearly seven months of continued running, eating right, and exercise she was looking better than ever. She had lost nearly fifty pounds. She got rid of the dark glasses, the extra baggy jeans, and over-sized sweat shirt. She now did her hair and even put a little make up on every so often. Today she woke up knowing that Covey was leaving. He was back off to New Jersey and traveling the world. He had came over right on time like he always did. The sun was shining beautifully and the warmth from the sun sent a relaxing sensation through her body. She greeted Covert with a reassured smile. Together they walked though the projects of Harvey. She felt with each step she took, every car that passed by and every person that looked in her direction, no one could look at her and see a joke. The two exchanged meaningless conversation for almost an hour in an attempt to avoid admitting that this would be their last meeting.

"Well, it's about that time for me to get going," Covert said reluctantly.

"I know."

"Anything you would like to tell me before I head off."

"No." She managed to say under her breath but her thoughts were racing dramatically. *Please don't leave . . . I love you . . . Thank you for everything.*

"Okay." Covey walked her to her door and headed out. He said good bye and started his walk down the street. He was a block down before he heard someone screaming.

"Covey! Wait! I have to tell you something!" She finally caught up to him and took a second to catch her breath. "Listen . . . I just want to say thank you for everything. I am going to miss you more than you'll ever know. I love you with all my heart, and guess what? I AM WORHTY!"

Covert smiled and gave her big hug. "Remember distance does not separate us it only creates more paths and all paths of love lead straight to the heart. I love you, and never forget that you are worthy." Covert turned for the final time and walked away into the light.

She headed straight for the school. She started to run her laps. She didn't stop after the first, second, third, or even fourth. She ran seven laps that day. A lap for each month she got to spend with a person she could only describe as her angel. The sun was setting as she stretched up to the sky. While she was stretching something caught her eye. Floating down to the ground was a square looking object. It landed next to a full green leaf in the field. She jogged over to pick it up. She stared aimlessly at it. A light breeze blew, seeming to catch her soul. She looked up at the sky inhaling the fresh air. As she clenched the picture in her hands, she half smiled at it. Then, she ripped the picture down the middle separating the familiar image of her and her father, once worn by Pooh. She admired the smile the little girl in the picture was giving her. Perhaps she thought that maybe it was not impossible to be happy. She gently placed that half of the picture into her pocket securing her own sense of hope. Then she ripped the other half into a heap of unrecognizable pieces releasing them from her grasp. She would never again allow her father to dictate her happiness. The pieces were picked up by the wind and got lost in the sunset.

CHAPTER 10—Reflections

(New York)

February 10, 2006

(Girl 2)

Her door opened slowly and in walked Little Bear. He was wearing the black dress shirt that his mom had picked out for him for the funeral. Clenched in his hands was his tie. He held it up and asked his sister if she could tie it for him.

"Come stand over here in front of the mirror and I'll do it for you." Together they stood in front of the mirror and she began to drape the tie properly around his neck. She was standing behind him and caught his eyes in the mirror staring at her.

"Why are you looking at me like that?"

"I'm just thinking about the last thing Nana said to me. She kept saying how much she loved me and all of us. I guess the thing I remember most was how she said pretty soon I am going to be the man of the house. That's a lot of pressure for a ten year old. I mean . . . I can't pay bills, and the only car I know how to drive is from Mario Kart."

"Little Bear I swear I wonder what planet you came from. Nana didn't mean that you literally have to take care of us. It is a figure of speech."

"Oh! I get it . . . so she figures because I'm smarter than you and got straight A's that I can do this."

She couldn't help but chuckle from such a crazy explanation. In fact it was the first time she had been able to laugh since the day she found out her grandmother had passed while she wasn't there to say goodbye. She tightened his tie and adjusted it by moving it from left to right. She looked at him through the mirror and smiled.

"Little Bear that's exactly what Nana meant when she told you that," she finally managed to say. Little Bear scurried out of the room. She took her time putting on her black dress as she looked through some old pictures from the albums. *Someday I am going to be happy again. Someday all this pain will go away. Nana I promise I'll make it through.*

December 13, 2006

She couldn't believe it had come down to this. She felt betrayed by her own mother.

"Listen I know you don't want to go in there, but I promise you she can help you. You are going through a lot right now and I know it's not easy, but it is for your own good."

"You don't know what's for MY own good. You don't know what it's like to wake up every morning and put up with the things that I do. Yeah, I am going to go in there, but I'm not going to say a word."

Before her mother could even say a word the passenger door had already slammed shut and she was at the door of the building. She signed herself in and waited to be called to go up and see her psychologist. It didn't take long before a skinny woman who looked to be in her forties approached her. She was wearing thick glasses and had a black blouse on. Her mouth had light wrinkles around it. The most intriguing aspect about her was her left eye had a dark scar that flowed from the top of her eyebrow all the way down to the start of her cheeks.

"Hello," the lady said, eagerly extending her hand, "My name is Dr. Maddie and I am the child and youth psychologist here at Go Girls Generation. I would love if you followed me to my office, and we can both get comfortable."

She followed Dr. Maddie up to the second floor. As they walked through the halls many pictures of what appeared to be teenage girls lined the walls. In every picture Dr. Maddie could be found smiling side by side with one of girls. The last picture was of Dr. Maddie standing in front of the building posing earnestly in front of a sign that read CHANGE THE WORLD.

"Ah yes, that was the grand opening of Go Girls Generation. I opened this facility to help out young ladies who struggle in life."

Trying not to sound too sarcastic she responded with, "Interesting."

"Well, come into my office. You may have a seat wherever you would like."

She flopped down in the lazy boy chair and reclined it back. Her focus was locked on the ceiling once she noticed the interesting pattern on it. The ceiling had a design of overlapping squares and in each square there were numerous circles.

"Are you comfortable?" Dr. Maddie's voice was suddenly more soft spoken.

She thought to herself. . . . Of course I'm not comfortable. My mom thinks I'm crazy. My stupid dad left me and hasn't spoken to me in only God knows how long. My little brother gives me weird looks. My boyfriend abuses me and worst of all I lost my grandma. How could you ask such a dumb question? Of course I'm not, geez. She smiled up at the ceiling counting the circles inside the squares and deliberately responded, "Yes."

"Okay for now I would just like you to relax. You may close your eyes and drift away. Get lost in your own world of thoughts. If there is anything you would like to share while you relax you may. Today we will keep it simple though."

I can't believe they managed to fit two-hundred and sixteen circles inside these squares. I wonder how much time I have burned counting these circles. I mean she can't keep me here forever . . . . What kinda psychologist lets you sleep the entire time . . . . I am so tired of this, but I know if I speak she is gonna wanna be best friends and try to get me to take a picture with her so I can be on her stupid Hall of Shame . . . . I bet I have like a million missed calls . . . Oh God, Mal is gonna get me good for this. While lost in her own thoughts of frustrations she blurted out, "Is true love suppose to hurt!?"

Dr. Maddie, surprised by the broken silence, looked up through her glasses and responded, "I don't think love is pain, but real love is a test of self interest."

She closed her eyes trying her hardest to suppress her tears and thought to herself, *then I am failing.*

March 30, 2007

Her visits with Dr. Maddie had continued. She began to trust Dr. Maddie and they made an agreement that every session she would be allowed to just let herself think and that when she was ready she would speak. There were still a lot of things that she hadn't told her though. She never spoke about Mal or the abuse. Most of their conversations stayed on the topics of her school work, her mother and Little Bear. Today she was scheduled to stop in for thirty minutes and talk about the week of school and start to plan goals for the month of April. It was after school so she dropped off her backpack and got in the passenger seat of the car. Her mom had always stayed silent on the drives, not really sure what to say to her daughter. She had always questioned herself. Was she was doing the right thing or not? It hadn't taken long for them to reach the building complex.

"Well, I'll be back to get you. Just call me when you're finished and, um, I love you." She leaned over to kiss her daughter on the forehead, but she had already exited the car and closed the door.

She was back in Dr. Maddie's office in her now favorite lazy boy chair. She always counted the circles inside the square. It was her favorite thing to do because in the midst of the silence it would take ten minutes to complete. That meant ten less minutes of having to expose the truth to Dr. Maddie.

"A new month is approaching and as always I would like you to think of some personal goals you would like to achieve. We haven't spent much time talking about your feelings of yourself and I would like you to start to consider that."

The sound of those words made her stomach churn. Dr. Maddie was closing in on her and she knew it wouldn't be long before she started asking personal questions. "How about make the honor roll!" she suggested to Dr. Maddie, as enthusiastically as possible trying to sound like that was what she really cared about.

"I love the way you think," A quick sigh of relief could be heard throughout the room, "but how about a goal targeted towards the people in your life; perhaps a better relationship with your mother and brother . . . or maybe meeting or letting go some of your old friends?"

The palpable silence that filled the room was soon broken by a ringing phone. She had forgotten to turn her cell phone off before coming up to the office. Dr. Maddie looked at her, bewildered, and asked if she was going to answer it. She already knew who was calling, and knew if she answered it Dr. Maddie would want to know who it was . . . especially if the conversation didn't go well.

"It's fine it's just a friend and I'll call him back later." Not even a second after she finished her sentence the phone rang again. Her attempt at looking reassuring faded along with the volume of the ringtone as she began to silence it.

"Seems to me that it might have been an important call? I feel that you may have not trusted yourself enough to answer it."

"Well nobody asked you and I can ignore any phone call I want to!" The edge in her voice sent a splitting echo off the walls.

"I am not trying to anger you. See this moment as an opportunity to trust yourself more. Please understand I am not demanding your trust for me. The trust you have in yourself is much more important."

"Take your bogus college talk and kick rocks," she blurted out. "I trust myself just fine and I don't need a pompous 'change-the-world-psychologist' or anybody for that matter to tell me I don't trust myself. I didn't want to come here anyway and I will not be back, so take a picture and frame that."

She stormed out of the office and slammed the door behind her. She darted down the stairs and into the main lobby. She reached the double doors and right before she kicked the doors open a poster above the doors read: **The curious paradox is that when I accept myself just as I am, then I can change. Carl Rogers**. The quote had been placed inside a picture of a giant clock. The hands of the clock all had the words change written inside of them.

She kicked the doors open and sat on the curb waiting for her mom to come pick her up. She checked her phone. There were thirteen missed calls all from Mal. An unread text message flashed across the phone. She read it with dread. *He is really gonna get me this time.*

April 6, 2007

It's my fault he had no choice. I guess this time I'll just say I had an allergic reaction. Her lies had become so convincing that it scared her. She had been avoiding him for more than a week now. She ran into him at Seven-Eleven while picking up a loaf of bread. She did her best to try to break the news to him easily. She wanted to be done with him. It is true she loved him, but she needed a break from this kind of life. He did not appreciate her actions at all. He lured her to his car promising that he would drive her home. They pulled up to her house and he explained how he wanted no problems. They had been together for nearly three years.

"I'm just tired ya know? I do love you, but you really hurt me."

"You can't forgive me for a couple of slip ups?"

"A couple? You made me make up excuses for every time you put your hands on me."

"Well guess what; here's another for you," and without warning he decked her clean across her mouth, "say you had an allergic reaction." It didn't take long for her bottom lip to swell. The metallic taste of blood was all too familiar to her. She got out of the car without a word. She headed towards the door and stopped in her tracks when he rolled down the window.

"Hey babe, tell me you love me."

On command she slowly turned around and in a shaken voice told him what he wanted to hear. He started to laugh out loud, but his laugh dulled as he looked up at the house and saw Little Bear staring out of the window at him. Their eyes met and with a dramatic pause, the stare became a piercing glare. Mal quickly rolled up his car window and drove off. Little Bear's eyes followed the car all the way until it vanished into the distance.

February 7, 2008

It had been two years since her grandmother had passed away. A series of events had taken place since then. She still hadn't quite found herself. There were many things she missed in her life. She missed her father. She missed her grandmother. She even found a place in her heart to miss that crazy Dr. Maddie and her world-saving self.

Today was special. She had come to the cemetery to deliver flowers to Nana. It was a chilly afternoon in New York. The wind blew wild as she and Little Bear walked up to the tombstone with the flowers in hand. She placed the bouquet of roses in front of the tombstone and traced her hands along the engraved words of the stone. She could feel her grandmother's presence.

Nana someday I am going to have the strength. I promise.

August 7, 2008

Her phone rang. Mal never called in the afternoon. He was supposed to be at work. She looked at her phone and managed to catch her breath. It was actually her best friend from New Jersey wondering if she was still coming over tomorrow. She had known Niya for years and she kept saying how excited she was to let her meet someone. She was excited and the trip to Jersey had been on her mind for quite some time because she needed to get away.

August 15, 2008

She had made it back to New York after spending some much needed time with her closest friend and the most happy go lucky person she knew. She was right on time to be welcomed by her boyfriend. His same old antics had not changed. They had spent most of the day together. She was feeling indifferent today. In fact she made up an excuse and told him that she was going to walk home. She was bracing herself for the blow to the stomach that she thought was sure to follow after she told him she was leaving. To her surprise he said nothing, and just took his hand and pointed towards the door.

It was a quarter to six and she began her journey back home six blocks away. The sun was beginning to set and the warm breeze lightly made her hair bounce with each step she took. Who needed a ride home on a day like this, anyway. She took interest in counting the sections of the sidewalk. She would count all the way to ten and then repeat the same process. As she rounded the final block leading up to her house the three little girls, Brenda, Brianna and Olivia waved their hands for her to come over to them. She smiled and pretended that she didn't understand their gestures. *I can't let them see me like this.*

She made it home and quickly raced upstairs and grabbed a paper out of her pants pocket. It was a number to someone she had met back at her visit to New Jersey. She pulled the number out and after several minutes of hesitation, she made the phone call to the stranger named Covey.

It wasn't long after she hung up the phone with him and she stood there staring in the mirror. Looking into the mirror she reminisced when she was four years old and her father and mother had been downstairs arguing. She was tucked in bed with her favorite teddy bear that her father had given her. She called the teddy bear Ten.

On her fourth birthday that had just recently passed her father had given her a small brown bear. At first she didn't think the bear was special. When her father had given it to her she pushed it away with her hands. He gave her a warm smile and told her why this bear was special.

"If you squeeze the bear and count to ten all your worries will go away; it is a magic bear." He hugged his daughter close with the bear held firm in his hand and counted to ten. His daughter looked up at him and smiled shaking her head and blinking her eyes in disbelief. To her amazement she felt rejuvenated and uplifted. At that moment ten became her favorite number.

Her mother and father went back and forth exchanging words she couldn't fully understand. She stood by her door and listened as she could hear the front door slam and her father never returned after that.

Snapping herself back to the present by seeing herself in the mirror, clearly not four years old anymore, she still couldn't help but stare in the mirror and count to ten. Her dark eyes were flooded with tears and she reached for the phone to make one final call.

"Hello," a tired voice came from the other end.

"May I speak with Dr. Maddie?"

September 29, 2008

Today would be her last visit to Dr. Maddie. They agreed to this final meeting so that she could clear her head and get things in perspective. She came into the familiar office and took her favorite seat for one last time.

"After today," Dr. Maddie began to speak, "you will have graduated from the Go Girls Generation program. I cannot express how proud I am of you, but please understand your final task has yet to come."

Dr. Maddie left the office and when she came back in she was rolling in a full-length mirror. She stood in front of the mirror and said, "I will begin the final task, and then you can follow."

Without warning Dr. Maddie took off her glasses and started to just stare in the mirror. The room fell still and Dr. Maddie began to speak loud enough so that her words could be heard, but not for the purpose of conversation.

"When I was seventeen years old," Dr. Maddie starting speaking while looking into the mirror, "I was in what I thought was the perfect relationship. He made me feel like I was worth something. He was my first love and promised he would take care of me. After a few short months things changed." Dr. Maddie's voice starting cracking and she could tell that Dr. Maddie was trying her hardest to fight back tears. "One night he picked me up from my house and bought me to some old run down shack that he claimed belonged to a friend. We went inside the small room and you could see the mice scurrying off as we entered."

Dr. Maddie looked down at the ground and stood on her tip-toes as if the mice might be in the office right now. "I had a gut feeling something was about to go wrong, but I decided to ignore it. He pointed to a small bed in the corner of the shack and told me to go lie down. When I chuckled at his demand things became intense and he grabbed me. He tossed me to the corner on top of the bed and started ripping away at my clothes. I reacted by slapping him in the face and he staggered back. He cursed me and on the floor he picked up some old charred wood and threw it towards my corner. The wood hit me directly in my eye and there was a nail still attached which slid down my face."

She touched her face as if remembering the sharp intense pain. She managed to sallow the lump in her throat and continued. "After he saw the blood he panicked. He thought I was going to tell on him and charged after me. I did what anybody would have done. I got up and ran out of the shack for my life. Of course I got away and he was charged on several counts and received only five years. If it hadn't been for my visible injury, I doubt he'd have gotten convicted at all."

Dr. Maddie moved from in front of the mirror and next to her. "I was very lucky to get away, but now you must get away. You need to look in the mirror and tell yourself your story. Then you too can break the bond that is holding you down.

She got up from the recliner and walked towards the mirror. Dr. Maddie moved away from her side and went over to her desk. When she looked up at the mirror she could see all the scars that had been left on her body. She rolled up her sleeves and the marks on her wrist had faded into long dark scars. She took her hands and wiped off the mascara. Her skin was dull and jagged. She focused her attention back into the mirror and in the reflection she saw her grandma to her right and Covey appeared over her left shoulder. They both smiled giving her a warm sense of security. She moved her eyes to look at herself, but instead, Mal was there. She moved her head in both directions hoping to dodge his reflection. It did not work. She quickly became flustered. A smug look crossed his face as the tears filled her eyes. He reached his hands out towards her.

Suddenly a confident smile came to her face. She began to reach her hand out towards him. He shook his head and winked. She thought to herself, *not this time*. She let out a fierce scream, picked up the lamp that was on the stand next to her and smashed it against the mirror. The mirror cracked such that a shower of glass from the mirror slowly started to fall to the floor. The reflection of him faded as the pieces of the mirror crashed to the floor. The last piece that broke off was of him with a dumfounded expression. She looked down at the damage she had caused. The mirror had broken into a million pieces and lay shattered on the floor. She noticed the plethora of pieces had somehow contained themselves perfectly into an empty square tile. She cracked a smile and started to count to ten.

Chapter 11—Tell the Truth

(Midlothian, IL)

March 28, 2006

(Girl 3)

She gave Lillian a kiss on the forehead. This was the hardest thing she had ever had to do in her life. She had to give her baby up. Lillian was only a few days old. Already she was a curious baby. Her eyes opened wide and her forehead was crinkled up as her mother held her tight. *This is for the best.*

Nurse Love stood with the back door of the car open. She had already bought the child a brand new car seat. She went over and gently took Lillian away from her and placed her snug in the car seat. She closed the door and looked up to the starry sky.

"You know what child," she began to speak softly; "I know what it's like to lose a child. I am a mother, too. You are better than me though, you decided to give up your child for all the right reasons, and I ran away from mines."

"Why did you run away?"

"I couldn't take care of her. I was too weak. I let my husband beat on me and I just had lost control. I wanted to escape, so I left my daughter behind in the pursuit to become a stronger person."

"Why didn't you ever go back to her?"

"I lost sight of why I left in the first place," she said raising her hands in the air, "I guess I forgot what freedom was. But then you came into that hospital room with that same look of fear I had. You reminded me so much of myself." There was a long silence that followed and Ms. Love continued with, "You reminded me so much of her, too."

"Ms. Love if you never had the strength to make it back to your own daughter how do you know I ever will?"

"Well, Lillian is a wonderful gift, and I have seen firsthand the connection you have had with her. Someday, and you'll know when, you'll tell your parents the truth about everything. Now, please get in the car. I will drop you off at home and then once things settle down with you and your family I will tell them that you had been staying with me. That way you can see Lillian whenever you want to."

It was the longest drive back home for her, knowing that she was about to give up Lillian. What if she really couldn't ever get her back?

Every few moments she looked in the back seat at her beautiful daughter. She thought of all the struggles she had been through up until that point. She remembered all the abuse and all the days she felt like giving up. She knew her parents would never truly understand. The car pulled up into her driveway and she looked at Lillian one last time and kissed her. She started back at Ms. Love trying her hardest to fight back the tears. She gave Ms. Love a big hug figuring she would never be allowed to see her again.

"Ms. Love I just want to say thank you from the bottom of my heart. I think I am ready to face the music now."

"You have all the information you need my child and you can reach me whenever you need me. We both will be waiting for you."

She got out of the car and headed towards the front door. As she reached the porch the light came on and a figure could be seen looking out the front window. The figure in the window jumped up and down and not even a split second later the front door opened. She was swept up off her feet and greeted with kisses from her mother. The commotion was heard and soon her father appeared in front of her. He took his glasses off and shook his head in bewilderment. He hugged his daughter and kissed her on the head. For the first time in months she felt secure.

April 1, 2006

She never told her parents about Lillian. She didn't have the courage to do so. Instead she fabricated a story about how she ran away and Ms. Love welcomed her into her home. Her parents never questioned her beyond that. They wanted her to feel welcomed and have a fresh start. She did lose all of her privileges though and was not allowed to leave the house unless her parents dropped her off. Today was going to be special. It was the first day she was going to see Lillian. She told her parents she found a full time job babysitting for Ms. Love. They agreed that she could do it because it was something constructive and would keep her off the streets.

The car pulled up in front of Ms. Love's house and she dashed out of the car and headed to the door. She introduced her parents to Ms. Love and walked into the house to get Lillian. It had only been a few days since she had seen her daughter, but it felt like an eternity. Her eyes were opened wide and it was the first time she had seen her baby smile as she lifted her in the air.

March 24, 2007

Lillian's second birthday had come quick. She was getting big fast. She got see Lillian every day after school. Her relationship with her parents had also gotten better. Her father was dropping her off to babysit when he pulled the car over to the side of the road.

"Dad what are you doing?"

He was looking at her through the rearview mirror. His facial expression grew somber and he asked her, "Is there something you want to tell me?"

Her heart dropped and the lump in her throat made it hard to speak. "No dad, why do you ask?"

"I just feel in my heart that there is something different about you, but hey—if you say you are fine then I will leave it alone."

"Yes dad. I just feel like Ms. Love and Lillian are important and have helped me see the light."

He said nothing else as he turned the blinker on and headed back onto the road. He pulled up into Ms. Love's driveway and gave his daughter one final look as she got out of the car. Ms. Love and Lillian were already outside waiting. Lillian was wearing a delicate white dress with a crown on her head. She picked up Lillian and gave her a big kiss. Her father watched from the car with a raised eyebrow, but then smiled a faint smile as his daughter looked at him. He pulled out of the driveway and slowly drove away.

May 2, 2008

The doorbell rang and she put on her bunny slippers and headed downstairs. She opened the door and almost stumbled backwards when standing in front of her was her ex-boyfriend . . . Lillian's biological father.

"What are you doing here," she demanded.

"Is that any way to treat the love of your life? Listen I know you were pregnant. I came here from Indy to make sure you did the right thing. Now, where is the baby?"

"I will never forgive you for what you did to me, and you will never see her."

"Good. I don't want to see her. I just came here to let you know I will not be there for you. I just can't do it."

He turned and walked away. She stood irate at the door, but she said nothing. *Watching you walk out of my life is the best thing that could happen to me.*

September 1, 2008

The summer days flew by and September crept up fast. She had spent countless hours with Ms. Love and her baby girl. Lillian was growing up fast and acting like a tiny little grown lady. She loved to play dress up and could form little fragmented sentences like; *"oooh no no this," "shhh be cute,"* and her favorite was, *"love you."*

Her life revolved around her child, but she couldn't help but feel guilty for never speaking the truth. One day, back in the summer, she had attempted to sit her parents down and tell the truth that she really was Lillian's mother and Ms. Love had helped deliver the baby. Her parents had come home around four after shopping. She called them into the living room. They sat down on the loveseat staring blankly at their daughter.

"What's wrong honey," her mother said adjusting her bottom into the couch while trying not to spill her tea.

"Well, I have this friend," she spoke hypothetically because she could feel her father's eyes ripping away at her . . . "and," she continued refusing to look at her father, "she is afraid to tell her parents something very important."

Her father leaned forward on the couch almost making his wife knock over her tea and he spoke calmly, "What does that have to do with you?"

Her mother slapped him on the knee with a bent expression. "This is girl talk, and obviously she wants to know what she should tell her friend."

Dad leaned back in the chair and crossed his arms, "She shouldn't hide stuff from her parents because eventually they will find out," he said coolly. His words were followed by two more slaps from his wife to his knees.

"What your father means by that is that your friend should tell the truth. Think about it like this, your friend's conscience would be clear, they could work together to figure out a solution, and what if it is life changing in a good way?"

She shook her head in understanding. She wanted to tell her parents, but she figured she needed a little more time. She got up and gave her mother a hug and a kiss. Her father stood up tapping his foot on the ground. She turned her attention and went over to hug him, too. Her mother had already walked out of the living room and was down the hall with what was left of her tea.

As she went to let go from her father's hug he pulled her back in. He spoke in such a low whisper, but she was sure she could make out what he said . . . *the truth will set you free.*

September 8, 2008

A young man took a seat next to her. Lillian's mother turned to her left and gave him a small faint smile. He seemed like a pretty friendly guy. The smile he gave in return was such a nice smile. It caught her off guard, but she took it as a friendly gesture.

Class proceeded as the psychology teacher read out the agenda for the day. She rested her head on her desk and decided to close her eyes. It had been a long night yesterday as she stayed at Ms. Love's house until Lillian finally fell asleep, which was at one in the morning. She drifted off into dream world.

In her mind, the sand between her toes gently massaged every inch giving her feet a cool relaxing sensation. She was standing over Lillian smiling down at her. In her hands was a small pail and shovel. Lillian was patting the sand down in the pail using the shovel. The tide gently brushed up against the shore giving the feeling of moving without every taking a step. There were no other people on the beach except for them. The shore stretched across a vast amount of the beach leading to where the eye could only see sparkles because of the reflection of the deep blue water. She never felt more peaceful as the sun smiled down upon them. She picked Lillian up and kissed her on the forehead. Lillian smiled and started patting her on the back. She kept on patting her, but this time with a little more force. She tried putting her down, but she held on and continued to pat her on the back.

She opened her eyes and to figure out who was standing over her. As soon as her vision came back into full focus she could make out that the guy with the nice smile was in fact the one gently patting her on the back. The room was empty of other students, but her teacher stood at his desk stuffing papers into his bag. The teacher snapped at her.

"I will not tolerate sleeping in my class. I hope this does not happen again."

She picked her bag up off the floor and shook her head. The boy that woke her up had already left the room. She wanted to at least tell him thank you. She got up from her desk and headed off to her next class. *If only I could have dreamed for a little bit longer.*

September 9, 2008

It was the start of another day. She decided that she needed to concentrate more in her classes. Her friends Melanie and Jayden had caught up to her right before first period. They were exchanging light conversation on the latest gossip. Melanie always knew the latest on the word. She was probably the prettiest of all the friends that she had. Melanie was multiracial with Black and Puerto Rican parents, and had long curly dark hair. Her friend Jayden was a nice guy. He did kind of have a boring style in clothes and didn't care much about the gossip; in fact he only stuck around because he had such a crush on her. Melanie realized it, but of course she didn't notice his attention, with all she had to think about.

The bell rang and the halls were flooded with students scurrying off to class. The trio of friends exchanged hugs and went their separate ways. As she turned around she ran into that guy from her psych class. He gave her a friendly smile.

"Um, hey thanks for waking me up yesterday," she said breaking the silence between them.

"It's not that big of a deal. You seemed so peaceful, and I really didn't want to bother you, but . . ." His voice was smooth and he seemed sincere as he smiled while the sentence trailed off.

"Yeah it was just a late night babysitting and all . . ." her sentence was broken by the sound of the bell. "Great. Now we are late."

"I'm sorry about that. You should head to class and you will see me around."

She fixed her lips to ask him why wasn't he coming to class, but her teacher was screaming her name down the hall in anger.

"First you sleep in my class and now you show up late!"

She rushed down the hall to head to the class. She looked back and saw the boy was already gone. *Lucky him,* she began to think, *not to have to go to class.* She walked into the class and took her seat. Waiting on her desk was a detention slip. Dayum. She couldn't catch a break today.

September 29, 2008

Melanie and Jayden waved her down all the way from the other side of the cafeteria. She smiled at her friends and headed towards their direction. The trio followed Melanie to the last available table in the cafeteria. They always sat at one of the better tables, which were round. But they were so late, only the neglected square tables were left. In one of the corner seats at a square table sat a full figured girl with a faded hooded sweater on. Melanie gave her a sarcastic smile and asked her to move down. Without a word the girl walked away and out of the cafeteria.

"Melanie would you be nice?" Jayden said under his breath.

"Not my fault she is having a bad day. Now, move Jayden because I want to hear more about this guy with the cute smile."

"I don't even know his name. We bumped in the halls a couple weeks ago and that's it. He doesn't even speak to me in class, he just gives me that big smile."

Jayden laughed and interrupted, "He probably thinks you the crazy one."

"Jayden shut up!" They both said at the same time. They all laughed.

The girls continued their mindless conversation and every so often Jayden would chime in with his cynical remarks. The lunch bell sounded ending lunch and the trio sighed and exited the cafeteria. The rest of the day was smooth. All she had on her mind was seeing Lillian after school.

It was Monday and that meant she had just spent the weekend with her daughter and Ms. Love. Three o'clock had come and she headed to her locker to put away her books and gather her homework. While putting away her books one of the pictures of her and Lillian hanging up in her locker fell off and hit the ground. Before she could even think about picking it up the guy from her psych class was already slapping the picture back in its rightful place. His presence had startled her, but she smiled at the gesture.

"That is a very beautiful child in the picture," he said softly.

"Thanks," she started back at him not sure how to continue the conversation. She would not have to say another word because he took over from there.

"Please accept my apology for my terrible manners. We keep bumping into each other, so it is only fitting that you know my name is Covey." He extended his hand out and shook hers.

"Well, nice to finally know your name." She introduced herself and somehow felt at peace finally knowing his name.

"I must be going now, so please excuse me I have a bus to catch."

She closed her locker and when she looked back up he had already drifted out of the doors. *Dag, that kid's so fast he must run track and what kind of name is Covey, anyway.*

September 30, 2008

She walked into her psych class feeling more confident than usual. She smiled at her new friend and mouthed the words hello. She took her seat and for the first time in a long time she felt more aware. She pulled out her syllabus and read over the agenda. The lesson today seemed fitting for all that was going on in her head. Today's lesson was the concept of positive psychology. When her teacher asked who wants to read aloud she raised her hand.

"Is that a stretch or are you really going to read to us?" her teacher said curiously.

"No, I really want to read today." She flipped open to the page in her book and began to read the passage aloud:

Positive psychology is a recent method of psychology which hones in on improving mental consciousness by focusing on talent rather than illness.

As she read each word she decided that this passage was speaking directly to her. She looked up when she was done reading and gave Covey a small smile. She took a special interest in the reading in hopes of finding a way to conquer her own problems.

Finally lunch time came and she met up with Melanie and Jayden. She explained to her friends how once again she bumped into that guy after school at her locker.

"So, you do like him?" Jayden asked, sounding heartbroken.

"I don't even know him he just makes me feel confident that's all."

"Whatever," Melanie interrupted, "Jayden and I are going to get a snack we'll be back and if Covey comes around no smooches allowed."

"Whatever." She watched her friends scamper off into the crowd. She focused her attention back on her disgusting tuna salad which seemed to talk back to her. She has half-way into a nibble of it when she felt the girl sitting far in the corner staring at her. She tried first giving her a smile of acknowledgment. It didn't work. She put the spoon full of tuna salad down and headed towards the girl. The closer she came to the girl the more she buried her head into a calculus text book. She was now standing over the awkward looking girl. Before she could speak a word a tap came on her shoulder. When she looked back Melanie was standing behind her tapping her foot.

"We're back and waiting on you. There is not a problem is there?" Melanie sounded as if she was going to do something about it even if there wasn't a problem. She looked at Melanie and Jayden and then gave one final glance back at the girl who was now looking out of the cafeteria window as if they weren't even standing over her the entire time. They started heading back to their seats and she gave one last look back at the overweight girl, and as they made eye contact she saw her mouth form the words, "I know him, too." She turned back around and took her seat at the table. *What did she mean that she knew him too?*

December 23, 2008

It was the last day of school before school would release for winter break. Nothing had changed in the course of the last few weeks. She still hadn't told her parents and she was starting to lose that confidence in herself. She and Covey had exchanged conversations on different occasions. Their talks always seemed to get interrupted or he would disappear after a short while. Despite not really knowing the guy, she felt like he seemed to bring something positive out of her. He made her feel secure somehow. She had shared different little things about herself and her life at home and he would follow it up by saying something positive. She was just about ready to tell him the truth about everything, but he did not show up on that day.

January 13, 2009 8:03a.m

It was going to be now or never. She smiled her good morning to him as he walked into the classroom. While the lecture proceeded she got out a piece of paper and wrote the note to him. As she watched him get up her heart dropped. This would be the first time she would tell anybody her story. She put the note on his desk and jetted out of the room. *There is no turning back now. It is time to take a stand. This one is for Lillian.* She made it all the way to lunch without passing out from the anxiety. Jayden noticed how pale she was and the fatigued look that had taken over her face. Melanie paused from the story she was telling and took notice of it as well.

"What's wrong with you?" Melanie asked, perturbed because her story had been interrupted. "Is this about Covey?"

She sighed audibly. "Yes. I told him something and I wish I hadn't."

"I am sure it will be safe with him," Jayden said in a coaxing voice rubbing her shoulder. "From everything you told us he seems like a nice guy." Melanie shook her head agreeing with Jayden to make up for the anger she caused.

"I hope so. I am going to the principal's office to go home early."

She hugged her two best friends and headed out the cafeteria. She went to the office and made the phone call asking her dad to pick her up. He made a promise that he would be there as soon as possible, but it wasn't looking good because his boss needed him to stay. She walked up to Ms. Iris, the school secretary, and asked if she could go to her locker and retrieve her things. Ms. Iris gave her the go ahead and she raced off to get them. When she reached her locker she noticed a white piece of paper was sticking out one of the top slots of the locker. She pulled it from the slot and it was an envelope. Written in perfect cursive on the front of the envelope read; My Wonder. She opened the envelope and read:

You will forever be my wonder. Is it not a wonder how you made it this far despite all that you have been through? Your story is truly one I have never heard. I am not sure how you could keep such a secret for so long without blowing up, but it takes true strength of character to reach out and ask for help. It is important that you know that you are not the one to blame in this situation. Your decisions were derived from fear and pure emotion. I knew from the first time I saw you that you had a heavy heart. Your eyes tell quite a story. It is time to set yourself free and break the silence in order to save your child. Your baby is waiting for you. I can sense your beautiful spirit and you have been waiting for this moment a long time. I believe in you and I love you for who you are, but more importantly I love you because you are about to conquer a fear that most spend their lives running away from; the truth. It's time for you to find your peace.

Agape,
Covey

She held the note clenched in her hands. Her tears had already hit the beautifully written note. She folded the note and placed it back in the envelope. She returned back to the office. Ms. Iris had a puzzled look on her face as to why she was crying.

"Dear, are you gonna be okay?" Ms. Iris asked, standing up out of her chair.

She smiled and looked Ms. Iris right in the eyes, "For the first time I think I am going to be okay, Ms. Iris."

Her dad came into the office and she ran up to him and hugged him. She left the school and got into the car. Her dad, playing catch up, got into the car too.

"That's how I know you sick," her dad said chuckling under his breath, "I haven't gotten a hug like that from you in a long time. It must be a high fever."

"Dad," she started as she buckled her seatbelt, "I need you to get mom from work, and then we have to go to Ms. Love's house." He looked at his daughter and his eyes began to water. "I know dad. Its finally time I tell the truth."

Chapter 12—Open Letter

(Portland, Oregon)

May 24, 2009

(Girl 4)

Dear Serenity,

I was thrilled to hear that your mother will be able to make it to your graduation. You have come such a long way in discovering who you are and who you want to be. Your journey has not been easy and full of uncertainty, but through it all you have proven that a person can make it out no matter how difficult the circumstances. I wouldn't be surprised if there were more wonderful things to come. As they say, good things come to those who wait.

I am excited to take a trip to see you soon. Please keep up the incredible work and I hope I will hear from you periodically with updates. You have my best of wishes and love.

Agape,
Covey

May 30, 2009

Dear Covey,

MY MOM CAME HOME!!! She surprised me yesterday when I came home after school. I walked into the door and she was sitting on the couch. I have never cried so much in my life. She thought I was going to hate her, but I forgave her. It was so good to finally hug my mother after all those years. We sat down and I caught her up on my life and how much I have grown.

When I asked her what she had been up to she shared the most intriguing story. She moved away to Illinois and became a nurse delivering babies. During one of her deliveries she met a teenage girl who had run away from home. She told me how she felt so bad and understood the pain the girl was going through that she decided to adopt the baby girl. The baby's name was Lillian and apparently they raised the baby together while keeping it a secret from the girl's parents. I couldn't believe my ears. They managed to do this for like three years, Covey.

I was curious to know what gave my mom the strength to come home. She told me that Lillian's mother had met someone who had changed her mind about everything. She gained the strength to tell her parents and they all sat down and had a big talk. So, my mother decided that if a young teenage mother could face the music why couldn't she? Covey, if it weren't for that guy that my mom kept calling an angel, she probably would have never come home. I guess that girl, my mom, and myself all found an angel. Thank you for being a part my life and giving me peace.

I know I love you without even knowing what you are like in person. I don't know what funny habits you have. I don't know what it feels like to look you in the eyes. The day I meet you my smile will never fade and that day, tears of sorrow will never escape my eyes again. I do know I will love you always and will eternally be grateful. I cannot wait to see you in 2012.

Love Always,
Serenity Love

CHAPTER 13—The Covert Peace

(Harvey, IL)

(Girl 1)

Reflection Assignment
English 101
Professor Woolfolk
October 2, 2009

I never felt that I would have a true friend. Yes, I did have friends in high school, but I did not consider them close. I was very closed up, and I never shared my feelings with anyone. In turn they never shared anything with me. Whenever I got close to someone they tended to hurt me or leave me. I had these walls, and they would ward off people. I use to put on a mean front to push people away, because I would rather hurt them than have them hurt me. I felt the whole world was out to get me. Every laugh and every comment I felt was aimed at me. I was behind this wall, and no one was there with me. Even the people I did associate myself with could sense this. I lost many people who could have been great friends. That just made me hate the world more. I was very insecure, pessimistic, and depressed.

When senior year rolled around, I was still all alone. It was me against the world, and I was losing. I spent my days within myself, and I soon became oblivious to what was going on around me. Day in and day out all things I did were almost robotic. It was like I was programmed to do the same thing every day. I would go to class, eat lunch, more class, then get on a bus to go home, and then I would lock myself away in my house, fearing any public interaction. One day, on the way home, it was a typical, with everyone else conversing with one another, and I sat there with a seat open as usual, never to be filled by anyone. On the left side of the bus a few seats up from me sat a guy. I turned again to look out my bus window, to watch the world that I felt was so cold pass me by.

Another day, I got on the bus and sat in my usual seat. Right before the bus was about to pull away, he walked onto the bus. The bus ride was always crowded, and the only seat that was left on the bus was the one that was next to me. He asked if he could sit with me, and I said yes. I did not answer much back, fearing that doing so would cause him to leave.

Almost every day after that he sat with me on the bus. We got to know each other really well and became great friends. We also hung out quite a few times to get to know each other better. Eventually, I learned a lot more about him, and he learned more about me. He had come from New Jersey, and was traveling to his mother in Portland.

He gave me some motivational speeches during our time together. His trademark speech would have to be his "I Am Worthy" speech. He gave me that speech and constantly reminded me to say those three words. It was hard to do because inside I did not feel I was worthy of anything. I felt I was not worthy of a better future, a happier life, or even him as a friend. It took me seven months to finally say I am worthy. I said it the day he left as I chased him down the street before he disappeared. He was certainly like no other. He was kind, patient, intellectual and philosophical. He pushed me to better myself. I sit here a better person and so glad I could call someone like him friend.

(New York)

(Girl 2)

July 11, 2009

Dear Covey,

I AM WORTHY! I have finally learned what those words mean. I have taken control of my life. I now have something to live for. I know my Nana is smiling down on me and I know she would be proud. I finally called it quits with my boyfriend. Of course he promised he would change, but I didn't fall for that this time. He decided to prove to me that he could and would change and he even took some anger management classes. Covey, even when he gets done he can never have me back. Despite all he has done to me I have found it in my heart to forgive him, but I will never forget what he did to me.

I am single and happy. I want to get ready for the real world and live my life to the fullest. I took a picture with Dr. Maddie, my psychologist, and it now hangs in the halls leading towards her office. I have gotten the other neighborhood girls to join Go Girls Generation, so that they too can learn how to love themselves and be powerful young women in this world. I am not sure why things happen the way they do, but because of you I have found a way to survive. I will continue to work hard. Thank you for all that you have helped me through. Every morning before I head out the door I look in the mirror and say "I am worthy." It is the most powerful thing. Thank you for giving me peace in my life.

I Love You

(Midlothian, IL)

(Girl 3)

May 19, 2009

Covey (My Angel)

You have changed my life. There is no doubt about that. Please continue helping people. You do an amazing job at it. I finally told Lillian about me. She had such a good reaction. I told her adopted parent about you and she called you the same thing I did, my angel. You are perfect. I know now because of you that you will change the world. I know growing up Lillian will hear stories about my angel. I hope that those stories give her inspiration, and help her make good decisions. I believe that even though you are not in her life that you will change her life as well. Because of you I made the decision to talk to my parents . . . They know about her. I made the decision to take her back. The day I turn eighteen I will have my daughter back. You changed that. You of all people were the one I thought about when I made this choice. Things have finally turned around for the better and I finally found someone who loves me just as I am and he was right in my face the entire time. I am happier than I have ever been. Thank you so much. You are the reason that I am still alive. You are the reason I changed my life. I love you.

Epilogue

Little Bear

Little Bear began to reassemble the stack of papers so that he could put them back into their envelope in the right order. He should have been tired, but his mind would not stop racing with all he had learned that day. It felt like he understood the word "mind-blowing" in a completely different way than he ever had before. He thought back to that morning, and how he thought it would be just another normal day. Boy, was he ever wrong. He finally understood the meaning of all of this. Each person he had read about, including himself, was in search of one thing, peace. We all want that in our lives, but we expect it to be paid in full, and appear to us all at once so that we can be sure we have reached that peace. The truth is, the little things create our peace, bit by bit. They are fleeting moments hidden among all of us, with small actions like a friendly smile or endearing words. Little Bear had finally figured out that the entire time Covey was coming here to see his mother, but along the way everyone's paths had crossed. He wanted this idea to live on forever. Little Bear finally knew what he had to do now, and realized he had to help spread the covert peace. He reached for the second envelope and couldn't help but wonder what paths he would cross next. A light summer breeze blew, sweeping a leaf across his feet. He turned the envelope over and opened it . . . .

READER'S GUIDE

This book may be interpreted and examined in various ways. The Reader's Guide is here to encourage discussion and critical thinking about the book among readers of all ages. We hope that this Guide will provide a solid jumping off place, from which you can journey as far as you would like go with the characters and themes in the book.

Section 1: Uncovering subtle plot points

There are a few things in the book that are either expressed in a very low key way, or are left open to personal interpretation. Here is some information that might take away any lingering questions for those who have not developed their own interpretations while reading the text.

1. Is Covey's mother alive?

    She has passed on. She is the person who has died in the plane crash, which is mentioned in the headline of a newspaper noted by Girl 3 as she buys a pregnancy test at the drugstore.

2. What did Little Bear wish for?

We leave the book not knowing for sure; we only know he made it, and Covey found it somehow. Most people feel strongly that they know what the wish was for, whether or not they agree on its actual content.

3. What is Agape, and why does Covey always use it in his letters?

Agape is a form of love that is unconditional, self-sacrificing, and thoughtful. It is a Greek word for one of the forms of love that does not involve physical attachment. It is considered by some to be the most pure kind of love there is. Covey is using it to express his deep affection without confusing anyone by implying that he is "in love" with them. That kind of love is not part of his agenda: he is all about agape love.

Section 2: Themes and imagery in the text

Several themes are woven throughout the narrative of the book. Some are associated with particular characters, but they seem applicable to many people in different contexts. When examining these themes, take the time to think about what they mean to you in your own life, too.

1. Why do you think the authors chose not to use names for the four main characters?

2. The authors use several kinds of imagery and analogies in the book, such as leaves, squares, etc. What do they add to the story? Do you feel any personal connection to these different symbolic representations?

Examples:

- Leaves falling and changing colors, how they look and what they might mean as they travel through their own leaf lives.
- Very small personal spaces, such as Girl 1's small bed and the way she adds to the lack of space by filling the bed with various stuffed animals, the most important one being Winnie the Pooh.
- Noticing patterns and counting things that appear in them, and what this might do for Girl 2. This includes her attachment to the number ten and the "empty" squares. Why ten? Why the see through squares that look empty?
- The little girl in the elevator. Who is she? Where is she going?
- There are lots of busses and mirrors in the book. Where do you see them? What do they mean? Does their meaning change depending on where you are in the book?

3. Death and relationships appear repeatedly for several characters. What message do you think comes from them? Do relationships have their own life-spans? Do people really leave us when they die? How do you think the characters would answer those questions during different parts of the book?

4. Relationship abuse is featured prominently in the book for several characters. It is still a growing phenomenon that couples face every day. Why do you feel abuse occurs in relationships? Do you think that human beings fear being alone so much that we will

sometimes endure certain pain to make sure someone will "be there" for us?

5. Little Bear takes on two roles in the book. He is both a supporting character and the narrator that frames the book for the reader. What do you think about Little Bear? Do you feel comfortable with him being the chosen narrator? Why/why not? What is the importance of the character Little Bear as a whole?

6. Do you think Ms. Love did the right thing by taking Lillian in as her own child? Could anything have gone wrong with the arrangement? How did each character take a leap of faith in order to make these arrangements? Can you imagine what would have happened if the arrangements did NOT work out as well as they did? What are some things that could have happened instead?

7. The authors decide to name the main character Covert, and nickname him Covey. The word "covert" actually means secret or hidden. Do you think it was important for Covert to remain a bit hidden? Why/why not? What might have happened if he was not so discreet and selective about his actions as he helped people?

8. Although there are many men and women who let people down in the book, the authors took care to include strong and positive adult male role models, like Mr. Chiphaliwali. Why is it so important that we see these kinds of males in action in the book? What roles do positive men play for their communities in the real world? Why is it more unusual to see the kind of nurturing these characters provide in men than it is in women? What can we do about it?

9. A lot of characters in the story find themselves alone and in tough situations. They tend to imagine they cannot move forward through it to something better, but they can, bit by bit. They also tend to feel like they are the only ones alone. Why is this? Do you believe that anyone is really ever completely alone? Why/why not? Furthermore, many people believe that having courage means not having fear. However, it really seems to mean moving forward even though you have fear. What role does this issue play in the lives of the characters in the book?

10. Many of the issues faced by the main characters in the book began during childhood trauma. Although this can be overcome, it can be challenging for many reasons. For example, many children do not feel empowered, and all of us pass through developmental stages where we believe in magical thinking. For example, a young school age child whose parents split up may truly believe that it is due to something s/he did wrong, because they think they have that magical power to control things. Do you think magical thinking plays a part in some of the story? Why/why not?

11. The ending of the story is very open. It is eventually revealed and assumed who Covert has been with from time to time, and who crosses his path. Covert walks away in the end, but the story never reveals what is inside the second envelope. What do you think is inside the envelope? Where do you feel the story ends, and why?

12. Given all the information that you have now gathered from the story, what do you feel "covert peace" actually is? What could it represent?

TARA N. WOOLFOLK, Ph.D., is a faculty member of the Psychology Department at Rutgers University—Camden. A native Delawarean, born in October 1965, she earned her doctorate in 2006 at the University of Delaware. Her teaching, research and personal interests include life span identity development, and personal and social adjustment. Often referred to by others as a warm and approachable person, she likes to think that it is important to model empathy and critical thinking in order to foster it in the lives of others. She has always had an interest in writing fiction in addition to her academic writings, and hopes this will be the first of many opportunities to use her professional training to think outside the box in a fictional context.